Nothing Josh had done, nothing he had achieved—not even a hastily conceived and swiftly regretted marriage—had ever dulled the memory of that one night he'd spent with Grace. Still, in his dreams, his younger self reached out for her.

It had been unbearably worse during the last twelve months. Sleep was elusive, and when he did manage an hour he woke with an almost desperate yearning for something precious, something that was lost forever.

This. This woman clinging to him. This child….

He brushed his lips against her temple and then, his head full of the warm, milky scent of baby, he kissed Posie—and for one perfect moment all the pain, all the agony of the last twenty-four hours, fell away….

Dear Reader,

I wonder how many publishing houses have become household names, where to say their names out loud conjures up an image so vivid that there is no need for explanation.

Only, I dare venture, Harlequin, which this year is celebrating its diamond jubilee—sixty years of entertaining readers with great stories and engaging characters in settings as familiar as small-town America and as exotic as a South Sea island. Stories that sweep the reader away on the wonderful roller-coaster ride that is falling in love. Emotional stories that touch the heart. Stories of honor and sacrifice that address problems as old as time as well as those that affect women worldwide in the twenty-first century.

As traditional as a fairy tale, as modern as Helen Fielding's Bridget Jones series of books.

Generations of women have loved these books, passed them on to their daughters, granddaughters and now their great-granddaughters, and I'm absolutely thrilled that *Secret Baby, Surprise Parents,* with its very modern solution to an age-old heartbreak, is part of this very special year.

Happy sixtieth birthday, Harlequin. May your diamond sparkle ever brighter.

Liz Fielding

LIZ FIELDING

Secret Baby,
Surprise Parents

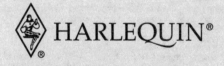

TORONTO • NEW YORK • LONDON
AMSTERDAM • PARIS • SYDNEY • HAMBURG
STOCKHOLM • ATHENS • TOKYO • MILAN • MADRID
PRAGUE • WARSAW • BUDAPEST • AUCKLAND

Recycling programs
for this product may
not exist in your area.

ISBN-13: 978-0-373-17579-6
ISBN-10:   0-373-17579-5

SECRET BABY, SURPRISE PARENTS

First North American Publication 2009.

Copyright © 2009 by Liz Fielding.

www.eHarlequin.com

Printed in U.S.A.

From bump to baby and beyond…

**Whether she's expecting or they're adopting,
a special arrival is on its way!**

**Follow the tears and triumphs
as these couples find their lives
blessed with the magic of parenthood.…**

**In May, Harlequin Romance® brings you
a whole month full of pregnancies and proposals,
motherhood and marriage!**

Don't miss:

With many thanks to Carol O'Reilly for her insight into the legal aspects of surrogacy in the U.K.

For more information visit www.surrogacyuk.org.

CHAPTER ONE

GRACE MCALLISTER restlessly paced the entrance to Accident and Emergency, punching yet another number into her cellphone in a desperate attempt to contact Josh Kingsley.

It would be Sunday evening in Australia and she'd tried his home number first. A woman had picked up.

'Anna Carling.'

'Oh…' The sound of her voice, the knowledge that she was in Josh's apartment answering his phone, for a moment drove everything else from her mind. Then, gathering herself, she said, 'Can I speak to Josh, please?'

'Who's calling?'

'Grace… Grace McAllister. I'm his…his…'

'It's okay, Grace, I know who you are. His brother's wife's sister, right?'

The woman was in his apartment and knew all the details of his personal life….

Grace gripped the phone tighter until it was hurting her fingers. 'Could I speak to him, please?'

'I'm sorry, Josh is away at the moment. I'm his personal assistant. Is there anything I can do to help?'

'Do you know where he is?'

'He's moving about a lot. Hong Kong. Beijing. Can I pass on a message?' she prompted when Grace didn't reply.

'No. Thank you.' This wasn't news she could ask a member

of his staff—no matter how personal—to deliver second-hand. 'I need to speak to him myself. It's urgent.'

Anna didn't waste time asking questions, playing the dragon at the door, but gave her a string of contact numbers. His cellphone. The number of his hotel in Hong Kong in case there was no signal. The private number of the manager of the Hong Kong office, since it was evening there. Even the number of Josh's favourite restaurant.

There was no signal. She left a message asking him to call her, urgently, then called the hotel. He wasn't there and the manager of the Hong Kong office informed her that Josh had flown to mainland China. Apparently Anna had already called the office and primed the manager to expect her call and again, when she wouldn't leave a message, he helpfully gave her the number of Josh's hotel there, and his partner in Beijing.

Beijing? He had a partner in Beijing? That was new since the last time he'd been home. Or maybe not. He hadn't stayed for more than a few hours and no one had been talking about business…

Calling the number she'd been given, she was told that Josh was out of the city for a few days and that the only way to contact him was through his cellphone.

She felt as if she were going around in circles, but at least it helped take her mind off what was happening at the hospital, even if she was dreading the moment she found him.

This time it rang. Once, twice, three times and then she heard him. His voice, so familiar, so strange as he briefly instructed the caller to leave a message.

'Miss McAllister…'

She spun round as a nurse called her name. Then wished she'd taken her time.

She'd been trying so hard not to think about what was happening to Michael. She'd only caught a glimpse of him lying unconscious on the stretcher while the emergency team worked on him before they'd rushed him away to the operating theatre and she'd been told to wait.

One look told her everything she needed to know. Her warm, loving brother-in-law had not survived the accident that had already killed her sister.

'Josh…' She forced his name out through a throat aching with unshed tears. There would be time for tears, but not yet. Not now. 'Josh… You have to come home.'

A day, even an hour ago, the very thought of seeing him would have been enough to send her into the same dizzy spin that had afflicted her as a teenager.

Numbed with the horror of what had happened, she was beyond feeling anything but rage at the unfairness of it.

Rage at the cruelty of fate. With Josh for being so blind. For refusing to understand. For being so angry with them all.

She didn't know what he'd said to Michael.

Remembered little of what he'd said to her, beyond begging her to think again.

All she could remember was his bloodless face when she'd told him that it was too late for second thoughts. That she was already pregnant with her sister's child. She would never forget the way he'd lifted a hand in a helpless gesture, let it fall, before taking a step back and opening the front door, climbing into the car waiting to take him back to the airport.

The nurse, no doubt used to dealing with shocked relatives, put her arm around her. Said something about a cup of tea. Asked if there was someone she could telephone so that she would not be alone.

'I've called Josh,' Grace said, stupidly, as if the woman would understand what that meant. 'He'll come now.' He had to come.

Then, realising she still had the phone clutched tightly to her ear as if she might somehow catch his voice in the ghostly static, she snapped it shut, pushed it into her pocket and allowed herself to be led back inside the hospital.

Josh Kingsley looked up at the majestic sight of Everest, pink in a freezing sunset.

He'd come here looking for something, hoping to recapture a time when he and his brother had planned this trip to Base Camp together. Older, a little wiser, he could see that it had been his big brother's attempt to distract him from his misery at their parents' divorce.

It had never happened. Now he was here alone but for the Sherpa porters, drawn to make this pilgrimage, take a few precious days out of a life so crowded by the demands of business that he was never entirely on his own. To find a way to come to terms with what had happened.

Now, overcome with the sudden need to talk to him, share this perfect moment, make his peace with the only member of his immediate family he cared about, he peeled off his gloves and took out the BlackBerry that he'd switched off three days ago.

Ignoring the continuous beep that signalled he had messages—work could wait, this wouldn't—he scrolled hurriedly through his numbers. Too hurriedly. The slender black miracle of computer technology slipped through fingers rapidly numbing in the thin atmosphere. And, as if he, too, were frozen, he watched it bounce once, then fly out across a vast chasm, not moving until he heard the faint sound of it shattering a thousand feet below.

When he finally looked up, the snow had turned from pink to grey and, as the cold bit deeper, he shivered.

Josh would come, but not yet, not for twenty-four hours at the earliest. Now, numb with shock, incapable of driving, she let the nurse call Toby Makepeace. He was there within minutes, helped her deal with the paperwork before driving her home to Michael and Phoebe's home and their three-month-old baby.

'I hate to leave you,' he said. 'You shouldn't be alone.'

'Elspeth's here,' she said, struggling with the simplest words. 'She stayed with Posie.' Then, knowing more was required, she forced herself to concentrate. 'Thank you, Toby. You've been a real friend.'

'I'm here. If you need anything. Help with arrangements…'

She swallowed, not wanting to think about what lay ahead. 'Josh will be here.' Tomorrow or the next day. 'He'll see to everything.'

'Of course.' He left his hand briefly on her arm, then turned and began to walk away.

Elspeth, a close friend of Michael and Phoebe, had answered Grace's desperate call and stayed with Posie. Now she said nothing, just hugged her and made her a cup of tea and then shut herself in Michael's study, taking on the task of calling everyone to let them know what had happened. She even rang Michael's parents—his mother in Japan, his father in France.

Grace had never met either of them—Michael and Josh had only minimum contact with either parent since their divorce—but Elspeth had at least known them, could break the news without having first to explain who she was. Then she stayed to answer the phone, field the calls that came flooding in.

Calls from everyone but the one person she was waiting to hear from.

Friends arrived with food, stayed to give practical help, making up beds in the spare rooms in the main part of the house while Grace did the same in Josh's basement flat. Even when her world was spinning out of control, she couldn't bear to let anyone else do that.

Then she set about putting her own life on hold, leaving a message on the answering machine in the self-contained flat she occupied on the top floor, before taking her laptop downstairs.

Sitting in the armchair that had been a permanent fixture beside the Aga for as long as she could remember, Posie within reach in her crib, she scrolled through her schedule of classes, calling everyone who had booked a place, writing the cheques and envelopes to return their fees as she went. Anything to stop herself from thinking.

After that she was free to concentrate on Posie. Bathing her, feeding her, changing her, shutting out everything else but the sound of the telephone.

She'd insisted that she tell Josh herself.

'It's night in China,' Elspeth said, after the umpteenth time the phone rang and it wasn't him. 'He's probably asleep with the phone switched off.'

'No. My call didn't go straight to the message service. It rang…'

'Asleep and didn't hear it, then.'

'Maybe I should have told someone in his office—'

'No. They've given you all the numbers they have and if you can't get hold of him, neither can they.'

'But—'

'You're the only person he'll want to hear this from, Grace.'

'Maybe.' Was she making too much of that? What did it matter who gave him the news?

'No question. You're the closest thing he has to family.'

'He has parents.'

Elspeth didn't bother to answer, just said, 'Come and have something to eat. Jane brought a quiche…'

She shook her head. 'I can't face anything.'

'You don't have the luxury of missing meals,' Elspeth said firmly. 'You have to keep strong for Posie.'

'What about you?' Grace asked. Elspeth had lost her best friend. She was suffering, too. 'You've been on the go all day and I haven't seen you eat a thing.'

'I'm fine.'

'No, you're not.' She lay Posie in the crib. 'Sit down. Put your feet up while I boil us both an egg.'

'Do I get toast soldiers?' Elspeth asked, managing a smile.

'Of course. It's my turn to look after you, Elspeth.'

'Only if you promise to take one of those pills the doctor left for you. You haven't slept…'

'I can't,' she said. 'Not until I've spoken to Josh.'

'But then?'

'I promise,' she said. And, because it was the only way to get Elspeth to eat, she forced down an egg, too, even managed a yoghurt.

She had a bath and might have dropped off in the warm water, but Posie was fretful. It was almost as if she sensed that something was out of kilter in her world and Grace put on Phoebe's dressing gown so that she would have the comfort of her mother's scent as she held her against her shoulder, crooning softly to her, walking the long night away—waiting, waiting, waiting for the phone to ring.

Finally, when she knew it was day on the other side of the world, she called again. Again, it was the answering service that picked up. 'Where are you?' she cried out in desperation. 'Call me!' All she got back was a hollow emptiness. 'Michael's dead, Josh,' she said hopelessly. 'Phoebe's dead. Posie needs you.'

She covered her mouth, holding back her own appeal. Refusing to say that she needed him, too.

She'd always needed him, but Josh did not need her and, even *in extremis*, a woman had her pride.

'Did Grace McAllister manage to get hold of you, Josh?'

He'd flown direct to Sydney from Nepal, stopping at his office to pick up urgent messages before going home to catch up on sleep.

'Grace?' He frowned, looking up from the list of messages his PA handed him. 'Grace rang me?'

'Last week. Sunday. I gave her the Hong Kong numbers but I knew you'd be on the move so I gave her your cellphone number, too,' she said. 'She said it was urgent. I hope I did the right thing.'

'Yes, yes,' he said, reassuring her.

Last week? On Sunday he'd been in the mountains, thinking about his brother. Thinking about Grace. There had been a message alert on his phone, but he'd ignored it….

'I dropped the damn thing off a mountain. Can you get me a replacement?' Then, 'Did Grace say why she was calling?'

'Only that it was urgent. It's the middle of the night there now,' she reminded him as he picked up the phone, hit the fast dial for her number.

'It doesn't matter. She wouldn't have called unless it was…' He stopped as the call went immediately to the answering machine.

"This is Grace McAllister. I'm sorry that I can't take your call at the moment. Due to a family bereavement, all classes have been cancelled until further notice. Please check the Web site for further details."

Bereavement?

He felt the blood drain from his face, put out a hand to grasp the desk. Posie…

It had to be Posie. Small babies were so vulnerable. Meningitis, cot death… After so many years of waiting, so much heartache.

'Cancel everything, Anna. Get me on the next available flight to London,' he said, dialling his brother's number.

Someone whose voice sounded familiar, but wasn't Michael, wasn't Phoebe, wasn't Grace, answered the phone.

'It's Josh Kingsley,' he said.

There was a momentary hiatus and then she was there— Grace, her familiar voice saying his name.

'Josh…'

It was all it took to stir up feelings that he'd done his level best to suppress. But this last year he hadn't been able to get her out of his head….

'Josh, I've been trying to get hold of you….'

'I know. I rang your number. Heard your message,' he said, ignoring her question. 'What's happened? Who died?'

He heard her take a long shuddering breath.

'Grace!'

'There was an accident. Michael, Phoebe… They were both killed.'

For a moment he was too stunned to speak. His brother was dead. 'When? How?'

'Last Sunday morning. I've been calling, leaving messages. When you didn't get back to me I thought… I thought…'

'No!' The word was wrenched from him. He knew what she'd thought and why, but it didn't hurt any less to know that she could believe him so heartless.

But then she already believed that.

She had been so happy that she was having a baby for her sister, couldn't understand why he'd been so desperate to stop her. And he hadn't been able to tell her.

'What happened?' he asked.

'The police said that the car skidded on a slick of mud. It went through a fence and then it rolled. It happened early in the morning and no one found them…'

'The baby, Grace,' he pressed urgently. 'Posie…'

'What? No! She wasn't with them. She was here with me. Michael and Phoebe were away for the weekend. It was their wedding anniversary but they left the hotel early. They couldn't wait to get back….'

Long before she'd stumbled to a halt, he'd clamped his hand over his mouth to hold in the cry of pain.

'Josh?'

'It's okay. I'm okay,' he managed. 'How are you coping?'

'One breath at a time,' she said. 'One minute. One hour…'

He wanted to tell her how sorry he was, but in a situation like this words were meaningless. And in any case she would know exactly how he was feeling. They were faced with the same loss. Or very nearly the same.

Grace wouldn't have to live with his guilt….

Instead, he kept to the practical. He should have been there to deal with this, make the necessary arrangements, but it had been over a week already.

'Who's with you? What arrangements have been made? When is the…' He couldn't bring himself to say the word.

'We buried them on Friday, Josh. Your father insisted on going ahead and, when you didn't call back, no one could reach you…' He heard her swallow, fight down tears, then she furiously said, 'Where were you?'

'Grace…'

He looked up as his PA returned. 'There's a car waiting to take you to the airport. You have to leave now,' she said, handing him a replacement BlackBerry.

'Grace, I'm leaving now for the airport.' Then, 'Keep breathing until I get there.'

Grace let Elspeth take the phone from her as she leaned weakly against the wall.

'Maybe you could get some sleep now,' she said gently, handing her the pills the doctor had left when he'd called after hearing the news. 'You've left plenty of milk in the fridge for Posie. I'll manage if you want to take a rest.'

'I know.' She put the pills in her pocket, knowing she wouldn't take them. She didn't want to go to sleep because when she woke she knew there would be a moment when she'd think it was just another day.

Then she'd remember and have to live through the loss all over again.

But she didn't say any of that. Instead, she hugged her and said, 'Thank you.'

'We're here, Mr Kingsley.'

Josh glanced up at the façade of the tall Georgian town house that Michael had bought when he had married Phoebe

McAllister. It was a proper family home with a basement and an attic and three floors in between. Endless rooms that they'd planned to fill with children.

Instead, they'd got him and Grace. A seventeen-year-old youth whose parents had split up and who, wrapped up in their own concerns with new partners, didn't want a moody cuckoo in the nest. And a fourteen-year-old girl for whom the only alternative was to be taken into the care of the local authority.

Exactly what every newly-wed couple needed.

They'd taken on each other's damaged siblings without a murmur. Had given him his own space in the basement, had decorated a room especially for Grace. Her first ever room of her own.

She'd been such a pathetic little scrap. A skinny rake of a kid, all straight lines when other girls her age had been testing out the power of their emerging attraction on impressionable youths. Only her eyes, a sparkling green and gold mix that could flash or melt with her mood, warned that she had hidden depths.

Like her nose and mouth, they'd been too big for her face. And, until she'd learned to control them, they'd betrayed her every thought.

Eyes like that should carry a health warning.

'Is there anything I can do, Mr Kingsley?'

Josh realised that the chauffeur—a regular who his PA had arranged to pick him up from the airport—was regarding him with concern.

He managed a smile. 'You can tell me what day it is, Jack. And whether it's seven o'clock in the morning or seven o'clock at night.'

'It was Tuesday when I got up this morning. And it's the evening. But I'm sure you knew that.'

'Just testing,' he said, managing a smile.

He'd counted every one of the last twenty-four hours as he'd travelled halfway round the world, coming to terms with the loss of his brother. And of Phoebe, who'd been the nearest thing to a big sister he'd ever had. By turns motherly, bossy, supportive. Everything that he'd needed.

Knowing that he would have to live with a world of regrets for the hard words he'd said. Words that could never be taken back. For holding on to his righteous anger, a cover for something darker that he could never admit to…,

But the hair shirt would have to wait. Grace needed him. The baby would need them both.

He climbed from the car. Grace's brightly painted 'Baubles and Beads' van was parked in its usual place but the space where he expected to see his brother's car was occupied by a small red hatchback that underlined, in the most shocking way, the reality of the situation.

Realising that Jack was waiting until he was inside, he pulled himself together, walked up the steps to the front door as he had done times without number to a house that had always felt as if it were opening its arms to him. Today, though, even in the spring sunshine, with tubs of bright yellow tulips on either side of the front door, it seemed subdued, in mourning.

The last time he'd been here he'd tossed the keys to both the house and his basement flat on his brother's desk—his declaration that he would never return. For the first time since he'd moved in here as a seventeen-year-old, he would have to knock at the door but, as he lifted his hand to the antique knocker, it was flung open.

For a moment he thought it was Grace, watching out for him, racing to fling her arms around him, but it wasn't her. Why would it be? She had Toby Makepeace to fling her arms around, to offer her comfort. At least she had the last time he'd come home on a visit. He hadn't been in evidence on the day he'd turned up without warning, but then discovering his girlfriend was pregnant with someone else's baby must have put a crimp in his ardour.

The woman who opened the door was older, familiar—a friend of Phoebe's. Elizabeth? Eleanor? She put her finger to her lips. 'Grace is in the kitchen but she's just dropped off. Try not to wake her. She hasn't been sleeping and she's exhausted.'

He nodded.

'You must be, too,' she said, putting her hand on his arm. 'It's a terrible homecoming for you. I'm so sorry about Michael. He was a lovely man.' She didn't wait for him to answer, just said, 'I'll go now you're here, but tell Grace to ring me if she needs anything. I'll call in tomorrow.'

'Yes. Thank you…' Elspeth. 'Thank you, Elspeth.'

He watched her until she was in her car, then picked up the bags that Jack had left on the top step, placed them inside and shut the door as quietly as he could. Each movement slow, deliberate, as if he could somehow steady the sudden wild beating of a heart that was loud enough to wake Grace all by itself.

He told himself that he should wait.

Go down to the basement flat, take a shower. But to do that, he'd need the key and the key cupboard was in the kitchen.

For the first time for as long as he could remember, he was frozen in indecision, unable to move. Staring down at the hall table where a pile of post—cards, some addressed to Grace, some to him—waited to be opened. Read.

He frowned. Cards?

He opened one, saw the lilies. *In sympathy…*

He dropped it as if burned, stepped back, dragged his hands over his face, through his hair as he looked down the hall. Then, because there was nothing else to do, he turned and walked slowly towards the kitchen.

He pushed the door very gently. It still squeaked. How many times had he heard Michael promise Phoebe that he'd do something about it?

He'd offered to do it himself, but Phoebe had just smiled. She liked the warning squeak, she'd told him. Liked to have something to complain about once in a while. It wasn't good for a man to believe he was perfect.

He could have told her that Michael didn't believe that. On

the contrary. But that had been a secret between the two of them and, somehow, he'd managed to smile back.

He paused, holding his breath, but there was no sound and he stepped into the room that had always been the hub of the house. Warm, roomy, with a big table for everyone to gather around. An old armchair by the Aga that the fourteen-year-old Grace had taken to like a security blanket, homing in on it when she'd arrived clutching a plastic bag that contained everything she possessed under one arm, a small scruffy terrier under the other.

The pair of them had practically lived in it. And it was the first place she'd taken the puppy he'd given her when old Harry had died a few months later and he'd been afraid her heart was going to break.

The puppy, too, had finally died of old age, but now she had a new love. Posie. The baby she had borne with the purest heart as surrogate for the sister who had given her a home and who was now lying, boneless in sleep, against her shoulder.

Michael, hoping that if Josh saw the baby he would finally understand, forgive him even, had e-mailed him endless photographs of Posie, giving him a running commentary on her progress since the day she'd been born, refusing to be deterred by Josh's lack of response.

There had been no photographs of Grace until the christening and then only in a group consisting of Grace, as godmother, holding Posie, flanked by Michael and Phoebe. A happy picture in which everyone had been smiling and sent, he suspected, with just a touch of defiance. A 'see what you're missing' message.

He hadn't cared about that. He'd only cared about Grace and he'd cropped the picture so that it was only of Grace and Posie. He'd had it enlarged and printed so that he could carry it with him.

Her face had been outwardly serene, but a photograph was just a two-dimensional image. It was without warmth, scent.

You could touch it, but it gave nothing back. But then it had been a very long time since Grace had given anything back to him. Keeping her distance, her eyes always guarded on his visits home.

At least he'd had time to get over his shock that, some time in the last year, she'd cut her beautiful long hair into a short elfin style. He'd come to terms with the fact that her boyish figure had finally filled out in lush womanly curves.

But this scene was not a photograph.

This was an intimate view of motherhood as only a husband, a father would see it and he stood perfectly still, scarcely daring to breathe, wanting to hold the moment, freeze this timeless image in his memory. Then, almost in slow motion, he saw the empty feeding bottle that had dropped into her lap begin a slow slide to the floor.

He moved swiftly to catch it before it hit the tiles and woke her, but when he looked up he realised that his attempt to keep her from being disturbed had failed.

Or maybe not. Her eyes were open and she was looking at him, but she wasn't truly awake. She wasn't seeing him. He froze, holding his breath, willing her to close them again and drift back off to sleep.

She stirred. 'Michael?' she said.

Not quite seeing him, not yet remembering. Still he hoped...

She blinked, focused, frowned.

He saw the exact moment when it all came flooding back, and instinctively reached out to her as he had a year ago. As if he could somehow stop time, go back, save her from a world of pain. 'Grace...'

'Oh, Josh...'

In that unguarded moment, in those two little words, it was all there. All the loss, all the heartache and, sinking to his knees, this time he did not step back, but followed through, gathering her into his arms, holding her close.

For ten years he'd lived with a memory of her in his arms,

the heavy silk of her hair trailing across his skin, her sweet mouth a torment of innocence and knowing eagerness as she'd taken him to a place that until then he hadn't known he had wanted to go.

He'd lived with the memory of tearing himself away from her, fully aware that he'd done the unforgivable, then compounded his sin by leaving her asleep in his bed to wake alone.

He'd told himself that he'd had no choice.

Grace had needed security, a settled home, a man who would put her first while, for as long as he could remember, he'd had his eyes set on far horizons, on travelling light and fast. He'd needed total freedom to take risks as he built an empire of his own.

But nothing he had done, nothing he had achieved, not even a hastily conceived and swiftly regretted marriage, had ever dulled the memory of that one night they'd spent together and still, in his dreams, his younger self reached out for her.

It had been unbearably worse during the last twelve months. Sleep had been elusive and when he did manage an hour he woke with an almost desperate yearning for something precious, something that was lost for ever.

This. This woman clinging to him, this child…

He brushed his lips against her temple and then, his head full of the warm, milky scent of baby, he kissed Posie and for one perfect moment all the pain, all the agony of the last twenty-four hours fell away.

Grace floated towards consciousness in slow, confused stages. She had no idea where she was, or why there was a weight against her shoulder, pinning her down. Why Michael was there, watching her. Knowing on some untapped level of consciousness that it couldn't be him.

Then, as she slowly, unwillingly surfaced, he said her name. Just that.

'Grace…'

Exactly as he had once, years and years ago, before gath-

ering her up in his arms. And she knew that it wasn't Michael,
it was Josh. Josh who had his arms around her, was holding
her as if he'd never let her go. A rerun of every dream she'd
had since he'd walked out of her life, gone away ten years ago
without a word, leaving a vast, gaping hole in her world. And
she clung to him, needing the comfort of his physical closeness. Just needing him.

She felt the touch of his lips against her hair as he kissed her.
The warmth of his mouth, his breath against her temple. And
then she was looking up at him and he was kissing her as he
had done every night of her life in dreams that gave her no peace.

There was the same shocked surprise that had them drawing back to stare at one another ten years ago, as if suddenly
everything made sense, before they had come together with
a sudden desperate urgency, his mouth branding her as his
own, the heat of their passion fusing them forever as one. A
heat that had been followed by ten years of ice....

Now, as then, it was the only thing in the world that she
wanted.

It was so long since he'd held her.

Not since he'd left her sleeping. Gone away without a
word. No, 'wait for me'. Nothing to give her hope that he'd
return for her. Not even a simple goodbye.

He had come back, of course, full of what he'd seen, done,
his plans. Always cutting his visits short, impatient to be
somewhere else, with someone else.

But she'd never let her guard down again, had never let him
see how much he'd hurt her, never let him get that close again.
She'd avoided the hugs and kisses so freely bestowed on the
prodigal on his increasingly rare visits home, keeping away
until all the excitement was over. Making sure she had a date
for the celebratory family dinner that had always been a
feature of his homecoming—because there had always been
some new achievement to celebrate. His own company. His
first international contract. His marriage…

Yet now, weakly, she clung to him, drinking in the tender touch of his lips, the never-to-be-forgotten scent of his skin.

Needing him as he'd never needed her. Knowing that even now, in his grief, he would be self-contained, in control, his head somewhere else.

He was holding her now, not because he needed comfort, but because he knew that she did. Just as she had all those years ago.

He'd hold her, kiss her, lie with her even if that was what she wanted. It was how men gave closeness, comfort to women.

That was all it had ever been, even then. When, after years of keeping her feelings to herself, doing a pretty good job of being the teasing friend who criticised his choice in clothes, girls, music, she'd finally broken down the night before he'd gone away—not to university this time, or on some backpacking gap year adventure with his friends—but to the other side of the world to start a new life.

Distraught, unable to express her loss in mere words, she'd thrown herself at him and maybe, facing the risk of the unknown, he'd been feeling a little uncertain, too.

She didn't blame him for taking what she'd so freely offered, so freely given. It was what she had wanted, after all. Had always wanted. Her mistake had been in believing that once he understood that, he'd stay.

He couldn't do it then and he wouldn't now.

He'd comfort her. He'd deal with the legal stuff and then, once everything had been settled, made tidy, the tears dried away, he'd fly off to Sydney or Hong Kong, China or South America. Wherever the life he'd made for himself out there in the big wide world took him. He'd go without a backward glance.

Leave her without a backward glance.

At eighteen she'd been so sure she could change him, that once she'd shown him how much she loved him he would never leave her.

At twenty-eight she knew better and, gathering herself, she pulled back, straightened legs that, curled up beneath her, had gone to sleep so that Josh was forced to move, sit back on his heels.

But, try as she might, she couldn't look away.

It was as if she were seeing him for the first time in years. Maybe she was. Or maybe she was looking at him for the first time in years instead of just glancing at him as if he was someone to be remembered only when he passed through on his way to somewhere else, forgotten again the minute he was out of sight.

She'd perfected that glance over the years.

Now she was really looking at him.

He seemed to have grown, she thought. Not physically. He'd always been a larger-than-life figure. Clever, with a touch of recklessness that lent an edge to everything he did, he'd not only dominated the school sports field but stood head and shoulders above the crowd academically, too.

He'd had those broad shoulders even then, but he'd grown harder over the years and these days he carried himself with the confidence of a man who'd taken on the world and won. And the close-clipped beard that darkened his cheeks—new since his last brief, terrible visit—added an edge of strangeness to a face that had once been as familiar to her as her own.

But this Josh Kingsley *was* a stranger.

She'd known him—or thought she had—and for one shining moment he had been entirely hers. But dawn had come and she'd woken alone, her illusions shattered beyond repair.

Older, wiser, she understood why he'd gone. That it had been the only thing he could do because if he'd stayed ten years ago, he would, sooner or later, have blamed her for his lost dreams. It was so easy for love to turn to hate. And nothing had changed.

He was home now, but once everything was settled, tidied away, he'd go away again because Maybridge was—always had been—too small for Josh Kingsley.

CHAPTER TWO

'GRACE,' he said, repeating her name. Calling her back from her thoughts, her memories. That was all. Just her name. Well, what else could he say? That he was sorry about his last visit? Sorry he'd got it all so wrong?

It was far too late for that and, without warning, she found herself wanting to slap him, yell at him for being such a fool. For staying away when coming home would have made his brother so happy. When it would have meant something.

'Where were you?' she demanded.

Josh shook his head. 'In the mountains. Everest. I was so close that I took a few days to go to a place with no work, no phone…'

He looked so desolate that she wanted to reach out and gather him close. Comfort him. Instead, she turned to the baby at her shoulder, kissed her precious head.

How two brothers could be so different—one gentle, caring, the other so completely cut off from emotional involvement—was a total mystery to her and falling in love with him had been the biggest mistake of her life. But, too young to know better, how could she have done anything else?

He had been her white knight.

Fourteen years old, in a strange town, faced with yet another school—when school had only ever been a place of torment—it could have been, would have been a nightmare if Josh hadn't ridden to her rescue that first terrifying day.

He'd seen her fear and, by the simple action of tossing her a spare crash helmet and taking her into school on the back of his motorbike, he'd turned her life around. He'd made everything all right by giving her instant street cred, an immediate 'in' with the cool girls in her class, who'd all wanted to know Josh Kingsley. And with the cool guys, who'd wanted to be him. At this school there had been no shortage of girls who'd wanted to be her friend.

Not that she'd been stupid enough to believe that she was the attraction.

She'd known it was Josh they all wanted to be near, but that had never bothered her. Why would it when she'd understood exactly how they felt? Not that she had worn her heart on her sleeve. A ride was one thing, but a sixth-form god like Josh Kingsley was never going to stoop to taking a fourth-year girl to a school dance.

She's almost felt sorry for the girls he did date. Each one had thought that her dreams had come true, but she'd known better. He'd shared his dreams with her and she'd always known that he couldn't wait to escape the small-town confines of Maybridge. Discover the life waiting for him beyond the horizon.

Not that it had stopped her from having the same foolish fantasies. Or, ultimately, making the same mistake.

Maybe he read all that in her face—she was too tired to keep her feelings under wraps—because he stood up, took a step back, placed the baby feeder he was holding on the table beside her.

'It was about to fall,' he said. 'I didn't want it to wake you. Elspeth warned me not to disturb you when she let me in.'

Too late for that. Years too late.

'Has she gone?'

He nodded. 'She said to tell you that she'll call in the morning.'

'She's been wonderful. She's stayed here, manned the

phones, organised food for after the funeral. But she's grieving, too. She needs to rest.' Not that Josh looked particularly great. He might have had the luxury of a first-class sleeping berth to take the edge off the long flight to London, but there was a greyness about his skin and his eyes were like stones. 'How are you?'

'I'll think about that later.'

'When you're back in Sydney?' she asked, reminding herself that this, like all his visits, was only a break from his real life.

'I'm not going anywhere,' he said. 'Not until everything is settled.'

'Everything?'

'I'm Michael's executor. I have to arrange for probate, settle his estate.'

'A week should do it,' she retaliated, and immediately regretted it. He had to be hurting, whether he was showing it or not. 'I'm sorry.'

'Don't! Don't apologise to me.' He looked up, took another deep breath. 'You and Phoebe were so close. She was like a mother to you.'

'A lot better than the real thing.'

'Yes.' He looked at her, and for a moment she thought he was going to say something she'd find hard to forgive. In the end he just said, 'Have you managed to contact your mother? Let her know what happened?'

She shook her head.

Her mother turned up occasionally, stayed for a week or two before drifting off again, a constant wanderer. Phoebe had bought her a mobile phone, but she had refused to take it and there was never anything as substantial as an address.

'There was a card from somewhere in India a couple of months ago. Whether she's still there…' She shook her head. 'Elspeth rang the consulate and she left messages with everyone who might be in contact with her, but she's even harder to get hold of than you.'

'I'm sorry, Grace. I flew back to Sydney from Nepal so I missed any messages you left at the office.'

'Nepal?' Then she remembered. 'Everest. What on earth were you doing there?'

'Making a pilgrimage.'

And if she felt lost, he looked it.

'I was going to call Michael, tell him I was looking at the sun setting on the mountain, but my hands were so cold that I dropped the phone.' He pushed his hands deep into his pockets as if, even now, he needed to warm them. 'We once planned to take that trip together.'

'Did you? I never knew that.'

He shrugged. 'It was when our parents first split. Before he met Phoebe.'

She frowned. 'She wouldn't have stopped him going.'

'Maybe he couldn't bring himself to leave her, even for a month. She was everything he ever wanted.'

While he'd had nothing, Grace thought. At least her mother did, occasionally, put in an appearance. It was disruptive, unsettling, but it was better than the nothingness that Josh had been left with when his parents had chosen to follow their own desires.

'Michael would have been happy to know that you finally made your dream trip,' she told him.

'Yes, he would. He wanted everyone to be happy. While I suspect all I wanted to do was make him feel bad…'

'No…' Her hand was on his arm before she could even think about it, but he stared at the floor as if unable to meet her gaze. 'Why would he feel bad? You were there. You were thinking of him.' Then, 'Did it match the vision?'

'The mountains were beyond anything I could describe, Grace. They made everything else seem so small, so unimportant. I wanted to tell him that. Tell him…'

'He knows, Josh,' she said, swallowing down the ache in her throat. 'He knows.'

'You think?' Josh forced himself to look up, face her. 'I

should have been here. I can't bear the thought of you having to go through all this on your own....'

'I wasn't on my own. Everyone helped. Toby was wonderful.'

Toby.

Josh felt his guts twist at the name.

Toby Makepeace. Her ideal man. Reliable. Solid. Always here.

'Michael's partners took care of all the arrangements for the funeral. And once your father arrived and took charge—'

'He's here?'

'He flew back straight after the funeral. There was some big debate at the European Parliament that he couldn't miss.'

About to make some comment about his father's priorities, he thought better of it. Who was he to criticise?

'And my mother? Has she raced back to the toy boy in Japan?'

'She's staying with friends in London.'

'Waiting for the will to be read,' he said heavily.

'Josh!' Then, 'She said she'd come back when you got here. I sent her a text.'

'I refer to the answer I gave earlier.' Then he shook his head. His issues with his family were solely his concern. 'I'm sorry. That was uncalled for.' He pushed his parents from his mind and said, 'Thank you for sticking with it, Grace. Not just leaving a message with the Sydney office.'

'I wanted to tell you myself, although if I'd realised how long it would take…'

'It must have felt like a year.'

'A lifetime.' Then, quickly, 'Your staff were terrific, by the way. Will you thank them for me? If I'd thought about it, I'd have anticipated resistance to handing out contact numbers to someone they don't know.'

'Of course they know you,' he said. 'Do you think I don't talk about you all?' Then, almost as if he were embarrassed by this brief outburst, 'Besides, they have an any time, anywhere list.'

'And I'm on that?'

'We both know that the only time you'd ever call me would be with news I had to hear.'

Once Grace would have laughed at that.

If only he knew how many times she'd picked up the phone, her hand on the fast dial number, not to speak to him, but simply to hear his voice. How she'd longed to go back to the way it had once been, when they had been friends…teased one another…told one another everything.

Almost everything.

'Grace—'

'I'm going to miss Michael so much,' she said quickly. Taking a step back from the memory of a night that had changed everything. When she'd thrown all that away. 'There wasn't a kinder, sweeter—'

'Don't.' He closed his eyes for a moment, then, gathering himself, he opened them and looked straight at her. 'Don't put him on a pedestal, Grace. Michael wasn't perfect. He had his faults like the rest of us.'

Grace was too angry to answer him. Even now he wouldn't let go of whatever had been driving him…

Instead, she held Posie close as she got to her feet, supporting her head with her hand. Then, when she didn't stir, she laid her in the crib beside her chair.

For a moment her tiny arms and legs waved as if searching for her warmth and her face creased up, as if she was about to cry. Grace laid her hand on her tummy until, reassured by the contact, the baby finally relaxed.

Once she was settled, Grace crossed to the kettle, turned it on, not because she wanted something to drink, but because anything was better than doing nothing.

'Your flat is ready for you,' she said, glancing at him. 'The bed's made up and you'll find the basics in your fridge. It's too late to do anything today and I'm sure you need to catch up on your sleep.'

'I'll hang on for a while. The sooner I slot back into this time zone, the sooner I'll beat the jet lag.'

'Is that right? As someone whose only trip overseas was the Isle of Man, I'll have to take your word for it.'

'The Isle of Man isn't overseas, Grace.'

'Isn't it?' she asked. 'I wouldn't advise walking there.'

That earned her one of those smiles that never failed to light up her insides and, feeling instantly guilty, she looked away.

'There's a casserole in the oven and I'm just about to eat. I'm not sure what meal time you're on but, if you're serious about keeping local hours, you'd be wise to join me.'

He shook his head. 'I'm not hungry.'

'Oddly enough,' she said, 'neither am I, but unlike you I can't indulge in the luxury of missing meals.'

She stopped herself. His body clock must be all over the place and while snapping at him might make her feel better, would certainly help distract her from an almost irresistible urge to throw caution to the winds, fling herself at him and beg him to make it better, it wasn't fair on him.

'Look, why don't you go and take a shower? Maybe have a shave?' she suggested. 'See how you feel then?'

He ran a hand over his chin. 'You don't like the beard?'

'Beard?' Under the pretext of assessing the short dark beard that covered his firm chin, cheeks hollowed with exhaustion, she indulged herself in a long look. Finally shaking her head as if in disbelief, she said, 'Are you telling me that the stubble is deliberate?'

And for a moment, just for a moment, his mouth twitched into a whisper of the smile that had once reduced the hearts of teenage girls to mush. If her heart-racing response was anything to go by, it had much the same effect on mature and otherwise sensible women.

But then she was a long-lost cause.

'I'm sorry, Josh,' she added. 'I just assumed that you'd forgotten to pack your razor.'

'If that were true, you'd have had no doubt about the beard, but I'm still carrying the bag I had with me in China and Nepal so I hope the washing machine is up to the—'

He broke off as a tiny mewl emerged from the crib. A tiny mewl that quickly grew into an insistent wail.

Grace sighed. 'I thought it was too good to be true. She's been so fretful for the last couple of days. Clingy. It's almost as if she knows there's something wrong.'

Josh took a step towards the crib and, very gently, he laid his hand, as she had done, on the baby's tummy.

Posie immediately stopped crying and, eyes wide, stared up at the tall figure standing over her. Then, as if demanding more from her uncle, she reached out a tiny fist and Grace caught her breath as Josh crouched beside the crib and touched her hand with the tip of one finger.

He'd been beyond angry when she'd told him that he was too late to stop the surrogacy, that she was already pregnant with her sister's baby. News that she hadn't even shared with Phoebe, determined not to raise false hopes until the doctor had confirmed it.

She hadn't known how he would react to Posie. As a youth, a young man, he'd been adamant that he would never have children of his own. His marriage to a girl he'd never even mentioned had been so swift, so unexpected that it seemed at the time as if everyone was holding their breath, sure that only the imminent arrival of a baby could have prompted it. But there had been no baby and within a year the marriage had been over.

Now, as he gazed down at this small miracle, she waited, heart in her mouth, for his reaction. For the inevitable question.

How could she do it?

How could she have felt the first tiny movements, watched that first scan, listened to the squishy beat of her heartbeat, cherished the baby growing inside her for nine long months, only to surrender her to her sister and his brother?

Other people had asked.

Not friends, true friends. They had understood. But a reporter from the local paper who'd somehow picked up the story had called her, wanting to know the whys, the hows, the financial deal she'd signed up to. If the woman had done her research, she'd have known that anything but expenses was against the law and Grace hadn't needed or wanted even that. It was the people who didn't know them who'd seemed most indignant that she could do such a thing. People who clearly had no concept of unselfish love.

None of those people had mattered, but she so wanted Josh to understand. Even though he disapproved of what she'd done, she needed him to understand, without asking, why she'd done it.

Don't, she silently begged him. Please don't ask….

'Michael rang me minutes after Posie was born,' he said, after what felt like an eternity. 'He was almost incoherent with joy.' For a moment he too seemed to find difficulty in speaking. 'I was in the back of beyond somewhere, the line was terrible but even through the static it came through loud and clear. His world was complete.' He looked up, looked at her. 'You gave him that, Grace.'

She let out a breath she hadn't been aware she was holding. He understood.

Then, catching up, 'Michael phoned you?'

'He didn't mention it?'

She shook her head. Why wouldn't he have told her? Had Phoebe known?

'What did you say to him, Josh?' she demanded.

'I asked him if you were all right and, when he assured me that you had sailed through the whole thing, I asked him if he was sure you had no doubts about giving up the baby. Urged him not to rush you…'

She waited, sure there was something else, but he shook his head.

'I didn't,' she said. 'He didn't.'

Why had it mattered so much to him? And why wouldn't they have told her that he'd cared enough to ask about her? Had been concerned that she was all right. Hadn't Phoebe known how much it would have meant to her?

Or was that it?

Had her sister suspected what had happened between them all those years ago? Had they been afraid that, in the hormonal rush after Posie's birth, a word from Josh might have been enough to change her mind?

Not wanting to think about that, she crossed to the crib, picked Posie up, cradled her briefly, cherishing the weight of her in her arms, the baby scent of clean hair, warm skin. Then she turned and offered her to Josh.

'Here,' she said. 'Take her. Hold her.' When he didn't move, she looked up to find him staring, not at the baby but at her. 'What?'

He shook his head. 'I thought you'd be married to your Toby by now, Grace. With a home, children of your own. Wasn't that what you always wanted?'

'You know it was.'

She'd wanted what her sister had wanted. A settled home, a good man, children. She also wanted Josh Kingsley and the two were incompatible. No one could have everything they wanted.

Her sister had never borne the children she had yearned for.

And she had never found anyone who could erase her yearning for a man for whom risk was the breath of life, the horizon the only place he wanted to be.

'Unfortunately,' she said, 'life isn't that simple.'

'Maybe men just have it too easy these days. All of the comforts with none of the responsibility.'

'Excuse me?'

'Well, it wasn't for lack of choice, was it? You appeared to be dating someone different every time I came home.'

'Not *every* time, surely?' Her well-schooled, careless tone was, she knew, ruined by a blush.

'You don't remember?'

She remembered.

Given a few days warning of his arrival, it hadn't been difficult to drum up some hungry man from the crafts centre who was glad of a home-cooked meal. Camouflage so that it wouldn't look as if she was living in limbo, just waiting for Josh to come home and sweep her up into his arms, tell her that he'd been a fool. Pick up where they'd left off.

These days, only Toby was left. He'd been brighter than most, quickly cottoning on to what she was doing and apparently happy to play the possessive suitor whenever Josh came home.

Why she'd still been going through the motions after so long she couldn't say. Unless it was because she still wanted it so badly. That it was herself she was fooling rather than him….

Whatever, she could hardly get indignant if he'd been fooled by her deception. Assumed that she'd fallen into bed with every one of them as easily as she'd fallen into his.

'Maybe they could sense the desperation,' she said, burying her hot cheeks in Posie's downy head, before holding her out to Josh. 'Here,' she said, placing the baby in his arms. 'Say hello to Phoebe Grace Kingsley. Better known as Posie.'

Josh held her awkwardly and Posie waved her arms nervously.

'Hold her closer to you,' she said, settling her against Josh's broad chest, taking his arm, moving it, so that it was firmly beneath the baby. 'Like this. So that she feels safe.'

She was desperately anxious for him to bond with this little girl who would never know her real father. For whom Josh, no matter how reluctantly, would have to be the male role model.

'She has a look of Michael, don't you think?' she suggested. 'Around her eyes?'

'Her eyes are blue. Michael has…had brown eyes.'

'All babies have blue eyes, Josh, but it's not the colour.' The tip of her finger brushed the little tuck in Posie's eyelid. 'It's something about the shape. See?'

She looked up to see if Josh was following her and found herself looking at the same familiar feature, deeper, stronger in the man. Remembered the still, perfect moment ten years ago when, after a long, lingering kiss, a promise that all her dreams were about to come true, she'd opened her eyes and that tuck had been the first thing she'd seen.

Josh felt as if he were carrying a parcel of eggs. Just one wrong move and they'd be crushed. Maybe Grace was just as anxious because she'd kept her arm beneath his, laid her long, slender fingers over his hand, as if to steady him.

This was so far from anything he'd imagined himself doing. He'd never wanted children. Had never wanted to be responsible for putting children through the kind of misery he'd endured. The rows. The affairs. The day his father had walked out and his mother had become someone he didn't know.

After a while, as he became more confident, Grace stepped back, leaving him holding this totally unexpected baby, who bore not the slightest resemblance to his brother.

If she looked like anyone, it was Grace, which was strange since she didn't much resemble her sister. He'd always assumed that they were half-sisters, although Michael had said not. The little tuck in the eyelid was familiar though, and he said, 'So long as she hasn't got Michael's nose.'

Grace laughed at that and the sound wrapped itself around his heart, warming him, and he looked up.

'I wish…' he began, then stopped, not entirely sure what he was wishing for.

'Michael never gave up hoping you'd turn up for the christening,' she said. 'He so wanted you to stand as her godfather.'

'He knew why I couldn't be there.'

'Too busy conquering the world?' Then, when he didn't answer, didn't say anything, 'Here, let me take her,' she said, rescuing him. 'I'll change her and put her to bed while you have a shower. Then we'll eat.'

He lifted his head and, glad of a change of subject, said, 'Actually, something does smell good. How long have I got?'

'Oh, half an hour should do it,' she said, not waiting to see whether he took her advice, but heading for the stairs and the nursery.

Josh let the shower pummel him, lowering the temperature gradually until it was cold enough to put the life back into his body, wake up his brain.

Doing his best to forget the moment when he'd come so close to breaking the promise he'd made to his brother. A promise he'd refused to free him from. Would never be able to free him from.

To forget the look on Grace's face as she'd looked up, and for just an instant he could have sworn that she'd seen the truth for herself.

He stared in the mirror. He favoured Michael—no one would have doubted they were brothers—but there were not by any means identical. Still he could have sworn she'd seen something.

He tugged on an old grey bathrobe that had been hanging behind the bathroom door for as long as he could remember, waiting for him whenever he was passing through London and could spare a little time to visit Maybridge, see his family.

He tied the belt and crossed to the alcove that still contained the desk he'd used when he was at school. Where he'd plotted out the future. Where he'd go. What he'd do.

His old computer was long gone, but the corkboard was still there. He reached over and pulled free a picture, curling with age, that Phoebe had taken of Michael and him building a barbecue in the garden years ago, when his brother had been about the same age he was now.

The likeness was striking, but Michael had more of their mother, her brown eyes.

He tossed the photograph on the desk and, turning to the wardrobe, hunted out a pair of jeans that weren't too tight, a sweatshirt that didn't betray his adolescent taste in music.

Then he checked his new BlackBerry for messages, replied to a couple that wouldn't wait. By then it was time to go back upstairs—to Grace, and to the miracle and disaster that was Posie.

Grace took her time putting Posie to bed.

She hadn't been so close, so intimate with Josh in years and she needed to put a little time and space between them. Get her breathing, her heart rate back under control.

She didn't hurry over changing her, washing her hands and face, feeding her little arms and legs into a clean sleep suit, all the time talking to her, tickling her tummy, kissing her toes. Telling her that she was the most beautiful baby in the world, just as Phoebe would have done.

Using the sweet little smiles to distract herself from vivid memories of Josh, naked in the shadowy light from a single lamp. His grey eyes turning molten as that first kiss had turned into hot, feverish, desperate need.

He'd been so beautiful. So perfect…

Posie waved a foot at her and she caught it, kissed it, peered into her eyes. Did all babies really have blue eyes? People said that, but was it true? Weren't Posie's a little bit grey? Then she saw the tiny flecks of brown and smiled.

'You're a beautiful, clever girl,' she said, doing up the poppers, then picking her up and nuzzling her tummy before putting her in the cot, 'and you're going to be just like your daddy.'

She carried on talking to her as she wound up the musical mobile, teasing, laughing and, once she'd set it gently turning, singing to her, very softly.

Upstairs, Josh stopped at the open door to his brother's small study. As always, it was immaculately tidy, with only his address book and an antique silver photograph frame on the desk.

He picked it up, stared at the picture of Phoebe cradling her new baby daughter. It looked perfect, but it was all wrong. A lie.

Even his perfect brother, who everyone had loved and thought could do no wrong, had one, unexpectedly human, frailty.

He carefully replaced the picture and left the room, closing the door behind him.

Later. He'd go through his papers later. Not that it would take long. He knew that all bills would be paid, life insurance up to date, will filed with the family lawyer.

Then he frowned. Had he changed it since Posie had been born? There hadn't been much time but Michael had never, in the normal way of things, believed in leaving a mess for other people to clear up. But playing fast and loose with life, keeping secrets, even with the best of intentions, had a way of coming back to bite you. And that tended to make things very messy indeed.

Whatever he'd done, it seemed likely that Grace would be the person most affected.

He wondered if she had the least idea how her life was about to change. How, on top of the loss of her closest family, she might also lose the home she loved. The baby who she'd so selflessly surrendered and yet hadn't totally surrendered, knowing that she would always be close to her. That she would still be hers to comfort. To hold.

He wiped those thoughts from his mind, took a breath, pushed open the kitchen door.

'Sorry,' he began. 'I had to make…'

He stopped. Looked around. He could have sworn he'd heard her talking to Posie but the kitchen was empty.

He shrugged, crossed to the cutlery drawer, planning to lay the table. He'd barely opened it when he heard her again. 'Night-night, Rosie Posie…' she said, laughing softly. 'Daddy's gorgeous little girl.'

He spun around, then saw the baby monitor on the dresser. Was it two-way? Could she hear him? No, of course not. But even so he stepped away from the drawer, planning to escape before she came down and found him eavesdropping on her private conversation with her baby.

There was the sound of something being wound up, the gentle tinkling of a lullaby.

'Night-night, sweetheart. Sleep tight…'

His imagination supplied the vivid image of her bending over to kiss this very precious baby.

And then she began to sing and nothing could have torn him away.

CHAPTER THREE

GRACE came to an abrupt halt at the kitchen door. The table was laid. A bottle of red wine had been uncorked. A jug of water beside it on the table. Everything ready for them to eat.

'Oh, Lord,' she said. 'Have you been waiting long?'

'I guessed you were still busy and made a start, that's all' he said, pulling out a chair. 'Sit down. I'll get the casserole.'

'No, I'll do that...'

'I'm here to help, not add to your burdens, Grace.' He picked up a cloth, took the casserole out of the slow oven and placed it on the heatproof mat. 'Did Posie go off to sleep?' he asked, looking up.

'Like a lamb. Until her next feed.'

'And when is that?'

'Whoa... Enough,' she said as he heaped the meat and vegetables on her plate. Then, answering his question, 'Around ten. There are jacket potatoes in the top oven.' She leapt up to get them, but he reached out and, with a hand on her shoulder, said, 'Stay. I'll get them.'

She froze and he quickly removed his hand. It made no difference. She was certain that when she took off her shirt, she would see the imprint of his fingers burned into her skin.

He turned away, took the potatoes from the oven, placed one on each of their plates.

'No—'

'You have to eat,' he reminded her.

'Yes, but…'

But not this much.

She let it go as, ignoring her, he fetched butter from the fridge, then picked up the bottle of wine, offering it to her. She shook her head and he beat her to the water, filling her glass.

'Michael told me that Posie was sleeping through the night,' he said when, all done, he sat down, picked up a fork.

'She was, but she's started waking up again. Missing her mother.' Then, not wanting to think about that, she said, 'Michael told you?'

'He e-mailed me daily bulletins. Sent photographs.'

Why was she surprised? That was Michael. Josh might have walked away, but they were brothers and he would never let go.

'He wanted you to share his happiness, Josh.'

'It was a little more complicated than that.'

'Your understanding, then,' she said, when he didn't elaborate.

'I understood.'

'You just didn't approve.'

'No.'

'Why? What was your problem?' She hadn't understood it then and didn't now. 'He didn't pressure me. Neither of them did. It was my idea. I wanted to do it.'

For a moment she thought he was going to explain but, after a moment, he shook his head, said, 'When did you have your hair cut?'

Her hair? Well, maybe that was better than a rerun of a pointless argument. Although, if the general male reaction to her cutting her waist-length hair was anything to go by, maybe this was less a change of subject than a change of argument.

'About six months ago,' she said, trying not to sound defensive. Every man she knew seemed to have taken it as a personal affront. She, on the other hand, had found it liberating. 'When did you grow the beard?' she retaliated.

'About six months ago.'

'Oh, right. It's one of those clever/dumb things, then.'

He thought about it, then shook his head. 'No. Sorry. You're going to have to explain that one.'

'Whenever someone does something clever, in another part of the world another person does something stupid to balance it out,' she said, as if everyone knew that. She shook her head and then, unable to help herself, grinned. 'Sorry. It's just a ridiculous advert on the television that drove Phoebe…' She stopped.

'Say it, Grace. Talking about her, about Michael keeps them with us.'

'That drove Phoebe nuts,' she said slowly, testing her sister's name on her tongue. How it felt. It brought tears to her eyes, she discovered, but not bad tears. Thinking about her sister being driven mad by Michael, them both laughing, was a good memory. She blinked back the tears, smiled. 'Michael used to tease her with versions he made up.'

'Like you're teasing me?'

'Oh, I'm not teasing, Josh. I'm telling it the way I see it.'

'Is that right? Well, you're going to have to live with it. But while I'm not prepared to admit that the beard is dumb, I have to agree that your new style is clever. It suits you, Grace.'

'Oh…'

She picked up her fork, took a mouthful of casserole. Touching her hair would have been such a giveaway gesture—

'I really, really hate it,' he added, 'but there's no doubt that it suits you.'

—and much too soon.

'Pretty much like the beard, then,' she said. And, since the food hadn't actually choked her, she took another mouthful.

'Grow your hair again and I'll shave it off.'

It was an update of the arguments they'd used to have about the clothes she'd worn. The girls he'd dated. The music she'd listened to.

'If you hold shares in a razor-blade company, sell them now,' she advised.

Perhaps recognising that step back to a happier time in their relationship, he looked up, smiled.

And it was as if he'd never been gone.

For a moment they allowed the comfortable silence to continue, but finally Josh shifted, said, 'Do you want to tell me about the funeral?'

She sketched a shrug. 'Michael and Phoebe had left instructions…' She swallowed. 'How could they do that? They were much too young to be thinking about things like that.'

'I imagine they did it for one another. So that whoever went first wouldn't be faced with making decisions. What did they want?'

'A simple funeral service in the local church, then a woodland burial with just a tree as a marker for their grave. I imagine that was Phoebe's choice. Your father wasn't impressed, but there was nothing he or your mother could do.'

'One more reason for Michael to lay it all out in words of one syllable.'

'Josh… He was their son,' she said helplessly.

'Not in any way that matters. His mother is living in Japan with someone she isn't married to. His father is in Strasbourg, raising his second family. He hadn't spoken to either of them in years.'

'You're their son, too. Have you spoken to them?'

'We have nothing to talk about.'

She said nothing. What could she say? That they had both been dealt rubbish hands when it came to parents?

In a clear attempt to change the subject, Josh said, 'How are you coping with your business? I heard your answerphone message cancelling your classes for the time being and obviously Posie needs full-time care at the moment, but what are you doing about the craft centre workshop? Private commissions?'

'Beyond asking someone to hang a "closed until further notice" sign on the workshop door?' she asked. 'Not much.'

'Have you actually been out of the house in the last few days? Apart from the funeral?'

She shook her head.

'Go into Maybridge tomorrow. Pick up your post, at least. You need to keep some semblance of normality in your life.'

'Normality?'

How on earth did he expect her to think about something as frivolous as jewellery at a time like this?

'It's all you can do, Grace. It's what Michael and Phoebe would want.'

Of course it was. She didn't need Josh to tell her that. But knowing it and doing it were two entirely different things.

'I'll drop you off there when I go into town tomorrow,' he said. 'I have to talk to Michael's lawyers. I spoke to them from the car on the way from the airport. They're expecting me first thing.'

'Right. Well, I suppose I should go to the workshop. Process what orders I can fill from stock, send notes to people about anything that's going to be delayed, give them the chance to cancel.'

'Maybe you should think about taking someone on to help out for the time being,' he suggested. 'Who takes care of things when you're gallivanting off to the Isle of Man?'

'I wasn't gallivanting. The craft centre received an invitation from a fair being held over a holiday weekend and a group of us went.'

'You're getting very adventurous.' Then, 'A group?'

'I wouldn't have gone on my own, but Mike Armstrong sent some of his smaller pieces of furniture, there was a candlemaker, Toby took some of his toys and one of his rocking horses and there was—'

'So who took care of the shop while you were away?' he asked, cutting her off.

'Abby. She started as one of my students. She's very gifted.'

'Then call her. You can't afford to turn down business.'

'That's the tycoon speaking. I'm sorry, Josh, but the world won't end if Baubles and Beads is closed for a few weeks. I promise you it's never going to trouble the FTSE 100.'

'No? You don't see yourself as a franchise operation with a shop in every shopping mall five years from now?' he asked, with a smile that she remembered from the days when he'd been planning to be the world's youngest billionaire.

Did he make it?

'Er… No.' She liked the way things were. Controllable. Totally hers.

'No surprise there,' he said.

Did he look a touch disappointed in her lack of ambition? He was the one who, when she had made jewellery for college fund-raisers, her friends, had pushed her into taking a Saturday stall at Melchester market. It was Josh who'd printed flyers on his computer, handed them out, called the local press who'd sent out a photographer to take pictures. He'd gone out of his way to prove to her that it wasn't only friends and family who would pay good money for something original, different.

'I'm not into mass production, Josh. People come to me because they know they'll never see anyone else wearing the same pair of earrings. The same necklace.'

'Then you need to find some other way to grow. A static business is a dying business.'

'Possibly, but not now.' Then she groaned.

'What?'

'I promised Geena Wagner that I'd make a wedding tiara for one of her brides. It's almost done. I can bring it home, finish it here.'

'No,' he said, and she looked up, startled by the insistence in his voice. 'I really don't think that's wise.'

'But Posie…'

'You need to keep your work and your home life separate.'
Again he had the look of a man with something on his mind.

'Easy to say. Elspeth would take care of her, but Posie
needs continuity, Josh. She's already confused. Leaving her
with anyone who has an hour to spare just so that I can keep
working won't do.'

'I know,' he said. Then, more gently, 'I know.'

'I suppose I could take her with me.' Was that his point?
That she was about to become a single mother with a business
to run and she needed to think about how she was going to
manage that. Answering herself, she said, 'I'd have to install
some basic essentials if it's going to be a permanent thing.'

'Like what?'

'You want a list?' she asked, smiling despite everything.
'How long have you got?'

'I'm in no hurry.'

'Do you have the slightest idea how much stuff a baby on
the move needs?' It was a rhetorical question and she wasn't
expecting an answer. 'Actually, I suppose I could ask Toby to
partition off the far end of the workshop so that I could turn
it into a little nursery.' Then, irritated at how easily he'd ma-
nipulated her into thinking about the future when she didn't
want to think about anything, she said, 'Okay, that's my life
sorted. Now tell me about yours. About Nepal. China. What
are you doing there?'

He began to talk about a major engineering project which
should have bored her witless, but just being the centre of his
attention, being able to listen to him without pretence was such
a rare treat that she didn't actually care what he was saying.

And when he turned the conversation to the jewellery-
making workshops she ran, showing a keen interest in what
she did, her stories about some of the odder characters who
came to them made him laugh.

He told her about places he'd visited, both fabulous and
foul. The wonders of the world, natural and man-made. The

remote, the exotic, the emptiness of a tropical beach lit only by the stars.

She told him about her recent trip to Brighton for a jewellery convention.

Finally, long after they'd finished eating, Josh stood up. 'It's late, you're tired,' he said, clearing the dishes.

She didn't bother to fight with him over it—he was right, she was finding it hard to stay awake—but instead rinsed plates and cutlery, stacking them in the dishwasher as he cleared the table. She wiped mats as he put away the butter, the wine. Their hands momentarily entangled as they both reached for the cruet and she found herself looking up at him.

'I'll take the pepper. You take the salt,' he said after a moment.

'No,' she said, pulling back. 'It's all yours, Josh. You're right. I'm done and by the time I've had a bath, Posie will be awake again, demanding food.'

'Are you okay up there by yourself now that Elspeth's gone home?' he asked. 'I could just as easily sleep in one of the spare rooms.'

'I'll be fine.'

He lifted a hand, laid his palm against her cheek. 'Sure?' he asked.

She swallowed. 'Really. Besides, if Posie is restless she'll keep you awake.'

'I have to fall asleep first. I'm going to look through some of Michael's things before I go down to the flat.'

'Right, but don't forget you're supposed to be working on UK time.'

He smiled. 'I won't.' Then, before she could move, he leaned close and kissed her cheek. 'Good night, Grace.'

'Um…good night,' she said, backing away until she reached the door, then turning and running up the stairs before she said or did something stupid.

She took a steadying breath before she glanced in at Posie and then, in the safety of the bathroom, she leaned back against the door, her hand to her cheek, still feeling the soft prickle of his close-cropped beard as it brushed against her skin.

Remembering the shock of his kiss as he'd woken her—when she was anything but Sleeping Beauty—knowing how easy it would have been for her to have asked him to stay with her. How easy it would have been to turn into his arms for the comfort they both craved.

Wondering what would it be like to lie beside Josh Kingsley on a white beach in the starlight with only the sound of the ocean shirring through the sand, the chirruping of tree frogs, the scent of frangipani on the wind.

He'd made it sound so magical. Doubtless it had been. And she wondered who had shared that tropical night with him?

He hadn't said and, unable to bear the thought of him with another woman, she hadn't asked.

He'd only once brought someone home. They'd been expecting him, but not the tall, tanned Australian girl he'd married without telling a soul. A girl who was, in every way, her opposite. Outgoing, lively, ready to follow him to the ends of the earth. Or so she'd said. It had lasted a little over a year. Since then he'd never brought anyone home, never even talked about anyone in his life, at least while she was around and although he was, by any standards, a rich and eligible bachelor, he didn't seem to live the kind of lifestyle that brought him into contact with gossip magazines. But just because he didn't date the kind of glamorous women who were pursued by the paparazzi meant absolutely nothing.

Only that he preferred to keep his private life just that.

Private.

She ran a bath, added a few drops of lavender oil. But even up to her neck in soothing warm water she discovered that once having thought about it, it was impossible to get the image of Josh, of her, their naked bodies entwined, limbs glistening in the surf, out of her head.

Horrified that she could be thinking about such things at a

time like this, she sank beneath the water in an attempt to cleanse the thoughts from her mind. Or maybe just to blot out everything. Only to erupt in a panic when she thought she heard Posie crying.

Her ears full of water, she couldn't hear anything, but when she threw a bathrobe around her and checked, she found the baby lying peacefully asleep.

She rubbed her hair dry, then eased herself into bed in the room next to the nursery. Closed her eyes and slept.

Josh replaced the telephone receiver in Michael's study, then opened the door, pausing at the foot of the stairs, listening. Everything was quiet. Grace couldn't have heard the phone—his Chinese partner hunting him down with impatient need to set up a meeting—or she'd surely have come down. Unless she'd fallen asleep in the bath?

The dark hollows beneath her eyes told their own story and, knowing he wouldn't rest until he'd reassured himself, he kicked off his shoes and, as quietly as he could, went upstairs. The bathroom door was unlocked. He opened it a few inches and said, 'Grace?' When there was no response, he glanced inside and saw, with relief, that it was empty. Then, as he turned away, he saw the nursery door was slightly ajar and, unable to help himself, he pushed it open, took a step inside.

He stood for a moment by the cot, looking down at the sleeping infant. Listening to her soft breathing, assailed by a torment of confused emotions as he considered every possible future. For Posie. For Grace.

Grace laughed as, her bottle empty, Posie turned to nuzzle at her breast, searching for more.

'Greedy baby,' she chided softly.

It was just getting light and, miraculously, they had both slept through.

She looked up as the squeak of the door warned her that she was no longer alone.

As Josh padded silently across the kitchen floor on bare feet, unaware that he had company, her first thought was that he didn't look so hot.

Then, as he reached the kettle, switched it on and stood by the window, staring out of the window at a pink and grey dawn while he waited for it to boil, she thought again.

He might have the hollow-eyed look of a man who'd spent the night staring at the ceiling but, in washed thin jogging pants and nothing else, he looked very hot indeed.

'Tea for me,' she said, before that train of thought joined last night's beach fantasy and got completely out of hand. Then, as he spun around, 'If you're offering.'

'Grace… I didn't see you there. Why are you sitting in the dark?'

'I've been feeding Posie,' she said. 'There's more chance that she'll go back to sleep if I leave the light off.' Then, 'Is the kettle playing up again?'

He looked at the kettle, which was clearly working, then at her.

'The one in your flat,' she said. 'Phoebe was going to buy a new one before…' Before the christening. But Josh had been 'too busy' to fly home, so she hadn't bothered.

'What? No,' he said. Then, 'I don't know. It was claustrophobic in the basement. Since I moved last year I've got used to seeing the sky when I wake up.'

'You have to go to sleep before you wake up,' she pointed out.

He shrugged. 'I managed an hour or two. I don't need a lot of sleep.'

'I remember,' she said.

'Do you?'

It was just as well the half-light was pink because she blushed crimson. That wasn't what she'd meant….

'I remember Michael saying that you'd moved to some

fabulous new penthouse with views to the end of the world.' They'd gone out there to visit, just after he'd moved in and BP. Before pregnancy. 'He said you wanted a closer look at all those horizons still waiting to be conquered.'

'Is that what you think?'

'I haven't the first idea what you want, Josh.' She shifted the baby to a more comfortable position, then said, 'So? What's it like?'

He regarded her for a full ten seconds before he turned away, dropped a couple of tea bags into two mugs and poured on boiling water. Then, his back to her, he said, 'It's like standing on the high board at the swimming pool without a handrail. You'd hate it.'

That hurt, cut deep, mostly because he was right, but, refusing to let it show, she said, 'I don't have a problem with views. I just don't have your unstoppable urge to find out what lies beyond them.'

'Still clinging to the safety net of home, Grace?' he said, lifting his head to challenge her.

'Still searching for something to cling to, Josh?' she came back at him.

He was the one who looked away and she realised that she'd touched an unexpected nerve.

'Will you stay and keep an eye on Posie while I go and take a shower?' she asked, easing herself to her feet, laying the sleepy babe in her crib, then fetching the milk jug from the fridge. 'Milk?' she asked, after fishing out the tea bags.

He didn't answer and, when she looked up, she realised that he was staring down at the overlarge dressing gown she was wearing, or rather at the way it was gaping open where she'd held Posie against her breast as she'd fed her from the bottle, as Phoebe had, giving the same skin to skin closeness as breastfeeding.

'This is Phoebe's,' she said, self-consciously pulling it

around her, tightening the belt. 'It's a bit big, but I've been wearing it so that Posie has the comfort of her scent.'

'Until yours and hers become indistinguishable?'

'No! It was just while she was away.' Except, of course, her sister wasn't ever coming back. 'I hadn't thought that far ahead.'

'No,' he said, with a heavy finality that suggested she hadn't thought very much about anything. 'Although I suspect that, unless her table manners improve, all she's going to get is the smell of stale milk or dribble.'

She frowned.

'There's a damp patch,' he said, then, when she looked down. 'No, on the other side…'

'Oh, nappy rash! I'm leaking.'

'Leaking?'

She opened a cupboard, grabbed a sealed pack of sterilised bottles. 'Make yourself comfortable. I may be a while,' she said, heading for the door.

'Wait!' He caught her arm. 'You're feeding Posie with your own milk?'

He sounded shocked. Instantly on the defensive, she said, 'Of course. Why wouldn't I?'

'You have to ask?'

Confused by his reaction, she said, 'Apparently.'

He shook his head. 'You're expressing your own milk, putting it in a bottle and then sitting down and feeding Posie with it. Do I really have to explain what is wrong with that picture?'

'There's not a thing wrong with it. Breast milk is the very best start for a baby. Everyone knows that.'

'In an ideal world,' he replied, 'but I suspect that precious few surrogate mothers stick around to play wet nurse.'

'I'm not!'

'As near as damn it, you are.'

She stared at him, shaken by the fierceness of his reaction. 'You know this isn't a normal surrogacy, Josh.'

'Really?'

How could anyone invest such an ordinary word with such a mixture of irony, disdain, plain old disbelief? Grace didn't bother to respond, defend herself, since clearly he was a long way from finished.

'In what way isn't it normal?' he asked. 'You're not married, so there was nothing to stop Michael's name being put on the birth certificate. I assume that happened?'

'Of course.'

'And presumably you went through all the legal hoops with the court-appointed social worker? Signed all the paperwork so that the Parental Order could be issued, along with a new birth certificate in which Phoebe and Michael were named as Posie's parents?'

'Of course. We were really lucky. It can take up to a year to get everything settled, but there was space in the court calendar and, since the social worker was happy, the paperwork was completed in double quick time.'

'So you are aware that you've surrendered any legal rights you had as Posie's birth mother?'

Grace clutched the plastic container of feeding bottles against her breast, a shield against words that meant nothing and yet still had the power to hurt her.

'You've done your homework,' she said, more than a little unnerved at his thoroughness in checking out the legal formalities. Trying to figure out what, exactly, he was getting at.

'I did, as a matter of fact,' he replied, 'although, since Michael explained everything in his regular progress bulletins, it was more for my own peace of mind than necessity.'

That was Michael, she thought. He would never have given up trying to make Josh see how perfect it all was. Trying to break down whatever his problem had been with this arrangement.

Poor Michael....

'So why are you asking me all this?' she demanded, making an effort to concentrate, trying not to think about what had happened, but how totally happy Michael had been. 'Since you already seem to have chapter and verse.'

'I just wanted to be sure that you fully understand the situation.'

'Of course I understand. And I didn't "surrender" Posie. She was always Phoebe's baby.'

'Truly?'

He slipped his hand inside the gown and laid his hand over the thin silk of her nightgown, fingers spread wide across her waist to encompass her abdomen in a shockingly intimate gesture. Her womb quickened to his touch, her breast responding as if to a lover's touch.

'Even while she was lying here? When you could feel her moving? When it was just the two of you in the night? You didn't have a single doubt?'

It was as if he were reading her mind. Had been there with her in the darkness, the restless baby in her womb keeping her awake, thinking about how different it could have been. How, all those years before, she'd longed for the protection he'd used to have failed, knowing that a baby was the one thing that would have brought him back to her.

She'd hated herself for wishing it, knowing how wrong it was to want a baby only to bind him to her. If he'd loved her, he would not have left. Or, if he had, would not have been able to stay away.

Knowing that carrying his brother's child for her sister was the nearest she was ever going to get to having Josh's child growing within her womb. But that was for her to know. No one else.

She knew she should move, step back, stop this, but the warmth, strength of his hand against her body held her to him like a magnet.

'Well?' he demanded, pressing her for an answer.

'No,' she mouthed, no sound escaping. Then again, 'No!' No doubts. Not one. 'It isn't unknown for a woman to carry a baby for her sister,' she told him. 'It was once quite normal for a woman to give a childless sister one or even two of her own babies to raise.'

'This isn't the nineteenth century.'

'No. And I've no doubt some of the neighbours believe I actually had sex with Michael in order to conceive but, since you've done your homework, you couldn't possibly think that. Could you?'

'Of course not—'

'Only, for your information, he was at a conference in Copenhagen when all the planets were in alignment but since the clinic already had his contribution in their freezer that wasn't a problem.'

'I know how it's done, Grace.'

'You have been thorough.'

'I didn't need to look that up on the Internet,' he said, his face grim now.

'No? Well, know this. Since I was here, living under the same roof, it made perfect sense to give Posie the very best start possible.'

'Did it? And whose idea was that? The whole breast is best thing.'

'Does it matter?' He didn't answer, just waited for her to tell him what he already believed he knew. And, infuriatingly, she couldn't deny it. 'Phoebe would never have asked.'

'No, I didn't think it was her idea. So how long had you planned to stretch it out, Grace? Six, nine months? Or were you planning to be one of those earth-mother types—?'

'That's enough!' she said, finally managing to step away from his hand. 'This wasn't about me. You told me that Michael was incoherent with joy. Well, I want you to imagine how Phoebe felt. After years of tests, hoping, waiting, longing for a baby of her own. The fertility treatment. All those failed IVF cycles. How do you think she felt when the midwife put Posie in her arms?'

'No one would deny that you did a generous, beautiful thing, Grace.'

'You thought I was wrong then and you still do.'

'No… Not you.'

'Michael, then?' Now she was confused. Who exactly did he blame for what had happened? 'Phoebe?'

'They were desperate. Beyond reason…' He shook his head. 'It no longer matters. All I'm saying is that it might have been better if you'd gone away for a while. Afterwards. Cut the cord, not just physically, but emotionally.'

He was so obviously concerned for her that she couldn't be angry with him.

'Or were you already planning to do this all over again a year from now so that Posie could have a brother or sister?'

She took a step back. He followed her.

'Are you really so terrified of getting out there and making a life for yourself that you were ready to settle for having a second-hand family? One without the risk of making a commitment to a relationship? Leaving the comfort of the nest?'

On the other hand…

'So what if I did,' she retaliated defiantly. 'What possible business is it of yours?'

'It's my business because, unless either of them left specific guardianship instructions,' he said, 'as Michael and Phoebe's executor, I'll be the one playing Solomon with Posie's future.'

She felt the blood drain from her face. 'What are you saying?' And then she knew. 'No. You can't take her from me. You wouldn't. She's mine….'

The words were out before she could stop them.

'I thought we'd just established that she's anything but yours. That you have no rights.'

'No…' It wasn't like that. Okay, so maybe he was right. Maybe she'd never given Posie up in the way that a true surrogate would have done. But she was her aunt. Her god-

mother. Obviously she was going to be close. Be there for her
if ever she needed her. And she needed her now. Then, more
fiercely, 'No!' she said again, this time with a touch of desperation. 'You don't want her! You couldn't even be bothered
to come home for the christening!'

He bit down hard, clearly fighting an angry retort. Then,
very calmly, very quietly, he said, 'Forget me, Grace. Where
Posie is concerned, I'm the last person you need worry about.'

Confused, she frowned. 'So what are you saying?'

Before he could answer, the phone began to ring.

Josh, closer, reached out and unhooked the phone from its
cradle on the kitchen wall, responding with a curt, 'Kingsley.'
He listened impassively for what seemed like forever, then
said, 'We'll expect you when we see you.'

'Who was it?' she asked as he hung up, turned back to face
her.

'My mother. Michael's mother—'

'Is she coming to see you?'

'—Posie's grandmother,' he said, his face set, his expression grim, 'who will be here some time this morning.'

On the point of objecting to his rudeness, she thought better of it. He clearly had something on his mind.

'Thank you. Now I'll finish what I was saying when the
phone rang.' He looked so angry, so fierce. 'When I was telling you that I was the last of your worries.'

'Last? When did you ever come last in anything?' she demanded.

Least of all where she was concerned.

'Last,' he repeated. 'I come a long way down the list of next
of kin. The only person who's lower than me on this particular list is you. After my father, my mother, *your* mother even…'

He let the words hang, giving her time to work it out for
herself. And, when she did, her heart stopped beating, her legs
buckled and there was a crash as the pack she was carrying
fell to the floor.

If Josh hadn't reached out and caught her, she'd have followed it but, his arms around her, he supported her, held her close.

'I won't let it happen,' he said fiercely, as she subsided weakly against his naked chest, a rock in a world that was disintegrating around her. Stroked his hand over her hair in a gesture meant to calm her. 'Trust me, Grace. Whatever it takes. You have my promise.'

The temptation to stay in the safety of his arms almost overwhelmed her. To call him on that promise. Leave him to fight her corner. But he wasn't always going to be around to make things right for her. If there was to be a battle, she would fight for her daughter. But she didn't think it would be necessary.

'It's all right, Josh,' she said, lifting her cheek from the steady beating of his heart, the warm silk of his skin. 'They wouldn't want her,' she said, looking up at him. 'They didn't want us.'

'No,' he said, his face grim. 'But then, neither of us had the legacy of a fine house, a couple of generous life insurance policies and whatever Michael's partnership in his architect's practice is worth. Even after the Chancellor has taken his cut in inheritance tax, it's still going to provide a very nice expense account for anyone who can prove their case for bringing up Posie.'

'What?' Then, 'Are you suggesting any of them would take her just for the money?'

'There are other factors. My father has a second family. A young wife. Three little girls who would no doubt welcome a baby sister.'

'But she's *my* baby!' The betraying words flew from her lips and in that instant she knew he'd spoken no more than the truth. She'd given her sister her baby, but she hadn't been able to totally let go.

'My mother would, I'm sure, give up her present precarious existence for this house, a steady income. She would, of course, employ a first-class nanny to take care of Posie. Might even offer you the job.'

Grace shook her head. 'She's mine,' she repeated. 'If it comes to a fight, any court would have to recognise that.'

He shook his head. 'I spent a long time last night researching this on the Internet. You carried a fertilised egg for your sister but, once you've completed the formalities, that's it. In law you're no more to Posie than her aunt. Nothing changes that.'

'No…' That small word held a world of pain, of loss. First her sister and now this. Then, as his words filtered through, she said, 'No. That's not right. You don't understand. I didn't… It wasn't…'

'What?' He was looking down at her, but now his forehead was furrowed in a frown, his grip tighter and, when she didn't answer, he gave her a little shake. 'It wasn't what, Grace?'

She looked up at him. She'd promised Phoebe she'd never tell, but her sister would want her, expect her to do whatever it took to keep her baby.

'It wasn't Phoebe's egg, Josh. It was mine.'

CHAPTER FOUR

'BUT...' Now it was Josh who looked as if he needed something to hold on to. 'They'd been going through IVF,' he protested. 'There were eggs available. Michael told me...'

'Michael...' She swallowed. 'Michael didn't know.'

Grace was propelled back by the shock that came off him in waves. She grabbed for the back of a kitchen chair, then sank down on it as her shaking legs finally refused to support her.

She gestured weakly at the chair beside her. 'Sit down, Josh.' He didn't move and she said, 'Please.'

For a moment she thought he was going to ignore her plea, turn around, walk away, just as he had when she'd told him she was pregnant with her sister's baby. That there was nothing he could do or say to stop her going ahead with the surrogacy.

And so he'd said nothing.

But, after endless seconds, he pulled out the chair beside her and sank down onto it.

'Tell me,' he said. 'Tell me everything.'

Grace looked across at the crib, then back at Josh.

'I couldn't bear to see what they were both going through after the failure of that last cycle, when the consultant called a halt, saying that Phoebe wasn't strong enough to go through any more.'

She reached out, wanting him to understand, but there was

something about the way he was holding himself, something so taut, so close to cracking, that she didn't quite dare cross that line.

'You have to understand how hard it was for them,' she pressed, wanting him to feel their pain. 'It was as if someone had died.'

'I understood,' he said tersely.

'Did you?'

Josh understood only too well.

Maintaining that cheerful, positive front for Phoebe had been tough on his brother. Michael had taken to calling him late at night when Phoebe had been asleep, pouring out his desperation, his sense of failure. There had been one call, when his brother had sounded so desperate that Josh had dropped everything and flown home, seriously concerned that he was on the point of a breakdown. Something Phoebe had been too wrapped up in her own loss to recognise.

Grace pressed him for an answer. 'Did you really, Josh?'

'I understood that it had become an obsession, that it was destroying them both,' he said. 'I wanted Michael to put a stop to it. Let it go. Adopt.'

'That seems such an obvious choice to the outsider,' she said. 'For a woman yearning for a baby of her own…' She let out a long shuddering sigh. 'I loved them both so much, to see them hurting like that was unbearable.'

'So it was you who suggested the surrogacy?'

'Not until I was sure it was a possibility. Like you, I did my research on the Internet, found a Web site run by and for people who'd already been through this. Then I saw my doctor, talked it through with her. Had all the health checks. I didn't want to raise Phoebe's hopes, not until I had the medical all-clear.'

'You should have had counselling. What if you'd found you couldn't give up the baby? It happens.'

'I know.'

'But then you weren't really giving her up, were you?'

She didn't argue. She could see how it must look to him,

but he hadn't been the one lying in the upstairs flat listening to her baby crying in the night, screwing the sheet into knots as she clung to the bed, waiting for Phoebe to call her, ask her to help. A call that she knew would never come.

'When I told them I was ready and willing to have one of Phoebe's fertilised eggs implanted, they both wept.'

'They didn't try to talk you out of it? Either of them?'

Her eyes flashed impatiently. 'Of course they did. Michael said that it was time for them to take the adoption route.'

'But Phoebe was hooked.'

'They weren't that young any more. We all knew that adoption would not have been easy. And I was absolutely certain that it was something I wanted to do.'

'So?'

'Michael had to go to Copenhagen to put in a bid for a new project. He said we'd talk about it again when he got back.' She shrugged. 'While he was gone, Phoebe and I went to see her consultant so that we'd have all the options when he got back. He gave it to us straight. While he was prepared to attempt implanting a fertilised egg, he didn't need to labour the point about how much harder it is to get a result that way.' She was staring at her hands. 'Phoebe had tried and tried, Josh. I'd seen what it did to her. Simple artificial insemination is much easier, much more reliable. By the time Michael came home, it was done.'

Josh rose slowly to his feet.

It was true, then.

Some sound must have escaped him, because Grace said, 'She's still Michael's baby—'

He shook his head and for a moment she faltered, but she quickly rallied and, on her feet, came back at him with a fierce, 'Yes! Posie is still just as much your niece as if Phoebe had given birth to her.'

'No…'

This time the word felt as if it had been torn from the

depths of his soul, as feelings that he'd battling with for a year threatened to overwhelm him.

'Please, Josh,' she said, her hand reaching for his, her voice urgent now, desperate. 'Posie needs you.'

'No!' His bellow, reverberating around the high ceiling, was echoed by a startled cry from the baby.

He was beside her in a stride, lifting her from the crib, holding her out in front of him at arm's length.

'Posie Kingsley is not my niece,' he said. Then, tucking the child protectively against his shoulder, he turned to Grace. 'She's my daughter.'

'What?'

'She's my daughter, our daughter.'

'No,' she said, shaking her head, taking a step back, looking for all the world as if she'd just stepped on the tail of a sleeping tiger. 'Don't…'

If ever her eyes betrayed her feelings, they betrayed them now. Then she turned away, as if she couldn't bear to look at him, walked to where she'd dropped the feeders and bent to pick them up.

'Give her to me,' she said.

'It's the truth,' he said, refusing to surrender Posie when, still not looking at him, she held out her arms to take her. He had to make her look at him. Had to convince her. 'Michael would have done anything and, God forgive me, I conspired in his deception.'

She let her arms drop, turned and walked out of the room.

'You can't hide from this,' he said, following her. 'Or bury your head in the sand. You're going to have to fight to keep your baby.'

She stopped at the foot of the stairs, swung around to face him. 'From you?' she demanded angrily. 'Is that what this is all about?' She gestured at the baby still nestled against his shoulder. 'Control of Michael's baby?'

'My baby. Why else would I have tried to stop the surrogacy? What I did, I did for Michael. To ease his torment. If Phoebe had become pregnant, if she'd had a baby, I could have lived with it. Been glad for them. But to know that you were carrying my child…'

'It was the same, Josh.'

'No, Grace. It was completely different. You were carrying my child. Have you any idea how that made me feel?'

That, at least, gave her pause. The anger died from her eyes, to be replaced by some other emotion. One that was far harder to read.

'How?'

'I can't explain…' It was true. There was no vocabulary for the anguish he'd felt, knowing that a woman he'd loved was carrying his child only to give it away. That she would never—could never—know the truth. He'd felt as if he were stealing something from her. Losing part of himself.

'Why didn't you just tell me, Josh? Instead of going on and on about what a fool I was. How I'd regret it.'

'Michael had made me swear…'

'On what? Your mother's life?' Sarcasm dripped from her tongue and he didn't blame her.

'Not even Phoebe knew,' he said.

'I don't believe you. He wouldn't have deceived her.'

'Just like Phoebe wouldn't have deceived Michael?' he retaliated, and colour streaked across her cheekbones. 'I warned you not to put him on a pedestal.'

'So you did.'

'If it helps, with Phoebe's history I didn't believe there was the slightest chance of her carrying any baby to term.'

'No, Josh, adding cynicism to deception doesn't help one bit.'

'No, I don't suppose it does.' Then, 'If it would have changed anything, despite my promise, I would have told you.'

'But I told you what I hadn't told them. That you were too late. I was already pregnant.'

He nodded.

'Maybe, if we hadn't jumped the gun, if we'd waited until he came home,' Grace said, 'he would have told me.'

'Maybe.' But, as their eyes locked, they both knew that it was never going to happen.

'But…' She shook her head. 'I don't understand. Why? Why would he do it? Why would you?'

'Michael was desperate and I had no choice.'

'They were both desperate, but there was no problem with Michael. It was Phoebe. They both knew that…'

'I know,' he said. 'I know. But while he was holding it together on the surface for Phoebe, he was perilously close to a breakdown. She was going through so much to give them both what they wanted. Michael felt so useless and that somehow morphed into the certainty that it was his fault they couldn't have children. I tried to get him to see a counsellor but he just begged me…' Grace was staring at him and he broke off, unable to continue. 'You're not the only one who owed Michael and Phoebe,' he said angrily. 'They took me into their home, too. I only did what you did, Grace.'

'You think?' She lifted one eyebrow. 'A few minutes in a cubicle with a magazine?'

'If you knew how helpless men feel,' he said. How helpless, how confused he'd felt, knowing that she was carrying a child he'd so unwillingly helped make. 'If I'd had any idea where it would lead, I'd never have gone through with it….'

Grace was in turmoil, couldn't begin to think straight, but one message was coming over loud and clear. That while he had been prepared to assist Phoebe to get pregnant, he'd flown half way around the world in an attempt to stop *her* from having his baby.

'It's okay, Josh. No need to labour it,' she snapped. 'I get the picture. Phoebe could have your baby, but I wasn't good enough.'

'No! That's not right. How could you not be good enough?'

'Then why?'

'Phoebe was just Phoebe. Michael's wife. You…' She'd never seen Josh struggle for words like this.

'What?' she demanded. 'How bad can it be?'

'Not bad. Far from bad, but we were lovers, Grace.'

'Lovers?' She'd never thought of them as lovers. 'Were we lovers?'

'I was the first man who knew you.'

First, last… She didn't want to think about how pathetic that was. 'I still don't understand what your problem was.'

'Don't you?' He looked at Posie for a moment, then back at her. 'My problem was that when Michael told me you were going to have a baby for Phoebe—not his, but my baby—it made me feel the way I did when I left you sleeping after the night we'd spend together, flying away like a thief in the night. I felt as if I was stealing your virginity all over again.'

'You didn't steal my virginity, Josh, I gave it to you with a whole heart, but we were never lovers.'

It struck her now so clearly. All those years she'd clung to something that had been unreal—nothing.

'To be lovers is more than sex. For lovers the whole person is engaged. Not just the body, but the head and heart. My head was missing that night and so was your heart. I don't believe you know how to love.'

She might as well have slapped him. Yesterday she'd wanted to, now…

Now she had to deal with the fact that it was Josh, not Michael who was the father of her baby. That it wasn't simple biology, a surrogacy without emotional involvement or ties, but that, ten years too late, her darkest dream had come true.

She didn't want to slap him, she wanted to hold him. Wanted him to hold her, tell her that it would be all right…

It was never going to happen.

He'd made his feelings plain. He hadn't expected or wanted this child. But then he'd once told her, when she'd found him burning photographs of his father, that he would never have children.

Later, when Michael and Josh had gone to the sports centre

to beat a squash ball to pulp, Phoebe had told her that there had been an announcement in *The Times* that morning, telling the world that his father's new young wife had just given birth to a baby girl.

'I have to deal with this,' she said, clutching the pack of feeders to her.

'You can't run away from this, Grace. Can't hide. Can't curl up in your armchair and make it go away. Posie is our daughter and we're going to have to sit down and decide what's best for her.' He looked down at the dark curls of the baby who was chewing at his shoulder. 'Make decisions that will alter all our lives.'

'She's Phoebe and Michael's daughter,' she replied, a touch desperately. She wasn't ready to talk about anything else right now. She needed time to come to terms with what he'd told her. That she'd had Josh Kingsley's baby. 'It says so on her birth certificate, as you've just taken great pains to remind me.'

'All the more reason…'

'No. You didn't want her, Josh. You never wanted her. You flew from Australia to try and stop her from being conceived.'

'And failed.' He came close to a smile. 'Not that I'm the first man to face that situation. Although I'm probably the first not to at least have had the fun of getting myself there.'

'Sorry, I can't help you with that one, Josh,' Grace said with a desperate flippancy that she was far from feeling. 'You'll just have to dig deep in your memory for consolation.'

'Not that deep,' he replied without hesitation, his eyes glinting dangerously as he lifted a hand to her face, ran his thumb down the side of her cheek. And for a moment all she could think about was how he'd kissed her—not ten years ago, but yesterday, when he'd woken her. Kissed her, kissed his baby. Because he'd always known that Posie was his. And now he knew that she was hers, too.

This was the first time either of them had ever talked about the night they'd spent together and Grace discovered that at twenty-eight years of age she could still blush like the shy fourteen-year-old who'd first come to this house.

Maybe Josh, too, was experiencing whatever similar response men felt when, without warning, they stumbled into emotional quicksand because, for a moment, neither of them spoke.

Then Grace said, 'You're okay, Josh. I don't have a father who cares enough to get out his shotgun and make you do the decent thing.'

'I know all about uncaring fathers, Grace. You're right. Having seen the dark side, fatherhood is not something I ever wanted, but here I am, like it or not.'

And Grace, who hadn't thought beyond the next hour for more than a week, realised that she had better start putting in some serious thinking time about what future she saw for Posie. For herself.

'This changes everything, doesn't it?' she said, sinking onto the stairs.

Josh sat down beside her, put his spare arm around her, pulled her against his chest. 'Everything,' he agreed.

They sat there for long minutes, both of them contemplating the future. Until last week, each had seen the road clear ahead of them. Two separate paths. One a quiet small-town road, the other a challenging climb up a twisting mountain path with the end lost in the clouds. Now their ways merged in a pothole-strewn lane that was shrouded in swirling mists.

It was Posie, waving a hand and grabbing a handful of Josh's hair, who finally brought them back to now, this minute and, as he yelped, Grace lifted her head, smiling despite everything as she rescued him from Posie's tight little grasp.

'Did she pull it out by the roots?' he asked, rubbing at his scalp.

'Not much. Get used to it.'

'Will you help?'

'I'm in it for the duration, Josh.'

And that, she realised, was all that mattered. She was now the only mother Posie would ever have and she just had to get on with it. If Josh wanted to be a father… Well, that was good, but she wasn't holding her breath.

And, with that, the world steadied and, realising that she was still clutching the feeders, she got to her feet. Milk. Shower. Work. Concentrate on one thing at a time. Do what had to be done and the rest would fall into place….

'I'll be as quick as I can,' she said, glancing down at him.

'You're leaving Posie with me?' She saw panic flash across his face. 'What do I do with her?'

She paused, the words *'Be a father'* burning in her brain. Not fair. She wanted him around for Posie, but she wouldn't stoop to blackmail.

He hadn't asked for—or wanted—this.

'Just keep her amused for a while,' she said, forcing herself to walk up the stairs, away from them. She got very nearly halfway before she looked back.

He hadn't moved, but was looking up at her, dark hair still ruffled from bed, ancient jogging pants sagging below his waist, exposing a band of paler skin, feet bare. Posie propped in his elbow, happily sucking at his naked shoulder.

If she had trawled her imagination for a perfect picture of fatherhood, she couldn't have bettered it.

Don't go there, she warned herself. It might only take one little tadpole waking up from deep freeze and eager to explore to make a baby, but being a father required a lifetime of commitment.

Josh thought one night made them lovers. He couldn't even stay married to the same woman for more than a year. He saved his energies for the really important stuff, like dominating his own field of engineering.

'Better still,' she said, a catch in her throat, 'let her amuse you.'

Josh looked at the baby, then back up at her. 'What does she do?'

'Do? She's not a performing seal.' Then, because he was clearly so far out of his depth he was in danger of drowning, she threw him a lifeline. 'She's just learned to roll over. If you put her down on the carpet, she'll show you.'

She didn't wait to see what he did, but ran up the two flights of stairs to her own flat, her brain pounding out the words *Josh's baby* over and over.

She'd been carrying Josh's baby inside her for nine months and not known. Had given birth to Josh's baby and had given her away.

How could she have done that?

How could she have looked at her and not seen? The little eyelid tuck. The grey eyes flecked with amber. A little curl that fell over her right eye.

He was right not to have told her.

To have known and have to give her up, even to her sister, would have been like tearing her heart from her body and, without it, she would never have survived.

Once she finished expressing her milk, Grace took a shower, then sorted through her wardrobe for something suitable for their trip into Maybridge, ignoring her usual bright colours as inappropriate, choosing the navy trouser suit she normally kept for visits to the bank.

She'd suggest walking into town. Apart from avoiding the hassle of parking, it would be good to stretch their legs, get some fresh air. They could cut through the park on the way home, maybe take some crusts. It was way past time that Posie was introduced to the joys of feeding the ducks. Phoebe had always loved doing that.

To the outside world they'd look like any ordinary family, she thought. Mother, father, baby. All they lacked was a dog.

She put her hand over her mouth, squeezed her eyes tight shut. Hung on until the urge to howl passed.

Grace's baby...

The words thumped through Josh's head as he took the stairs down to the basement flat. Last night he'd stood for a long time in the shadows of the nursery, watching his child sleeping, as every shade of emotion raced through him.

Anger, confusion, guilt. Grief at not just the loss of his brother and Phoebe, but of this last year when he'd walled himself up, unable to come to terms with what he'd done, what his brother had done. Feeling somehow cheated, used. Worst of all, having deep buried feelings for Grace stirred up to torment him.

The minute he'd stopped concentrating on something else, his mind would sandbag him with memories of how it had felt to be buried to the hilt in her sweet, hot body, her legs wrapped around him as she'd cried out his name. Creating pictures of her carrying his child, as if the one had led from the other.

He'd never wanted to be a father. No man had ever been more careful to avoid it. Even when he'd gone to that clinic, done what was necessary, he had managed to distance himself from the reality of it. Any baby would be Michael's, not his. And it had worked until he had discovered that it was Grace who'd be carrying his seed, at which point dispassion had deserted him.

Now, lifting his little girl from his shoulder, holding her in front of him, he was faced with more reality than he could handle.

'So, Posie,' he said, 'are you going to amuse me?'

Posie, head wobbling slightly, frowned in concentration as if considering his question, just as her mother had once frowned over her homework.

'Your mother said you can roll. Is that the extent of your repertoire?'

That earned him his first smile.

'What? You think that's a funny word, do you?'

Posie made a grab for his cheek, found the short stubble of his beard and tugged.

'Oh, no, you don't, young lady,' he gasped and, eyes watering, put her down on the carpet, pulled on the sweater he'd discarded the night before, then settled down on the floor beside her.

Posie stuck her fingers in her mouth and flung her legs up in the air.

'Oh, please,' he said. 'Is that any way for a lady to behave?'

Posie blew a bubble.

Grace put the feeding bottles in the fridge, laid the table for breakfast and then, since Josh and Posie had still not appeared, she went looking for them.

They weren't in the living room—the most obvious 'rolling' territory—or anywhere else on the ground floor.

The internal door to the basement flat was still open.

She crossed to it, but hesitated on the threshold. It wasn't that she never went down there. She had always volunteered to prepare it for him when he'd been expected home, whisking through it with vacuum cleaner and duster, checking the bathroom was stocked with everything he might need, the fridge contained the essentials. Smoothing Phoebe's best linen sheets over the mattress, fluffing up the pillows.

She had always avoided going down there when he had actually been in residence.

She'd even weaned herself off going down there once he'd gone, wallowing in the scent of him clinging to sheets, towels.

It had been years since she'd taken a pillowcase he'd slept on to tuck beneath her own pillow. Her own comfort blanket.

As she hovered at the head of the stairs, the rich, deep sound of his laughter drifted upwards and, drawn by this unexpected, wonderfully heart-lifting sound, she took one step, then another and then she was standing in the small lobby, looking through the open door into Josh's bedroom.

Unaware of her presence, he was lying face down on the floor, his back to her, playing peekaboo with Posie. Lifting the hem of the sweater he'd thrown on, hiding his face and then popping out with a, 'Boo.' Posie responded by throwing up her legs and wriggling with pleasure.

Josh laughed. 'Again?'

Posie waved her arms excitedly.

The two of them were locked in their own intimate little bubble, totally focused on each other. It was touching, beautiful, unutterably sad, and Grace was torn in her emotions, wanting to laugh with Josh and Posie and weep for Michael and Phoebe.

She did neither.

Instead, determined not to disturb father and daughter as they discovered each other, she clamped her lips together, took a step back, then turned and, as silently as possible, went back upstairs.

CHAPTER FIVE

JOSH couldn't have said whether it was a movement of air, some almost imperceptible sound or something else, but he looked over his shoulder, certain that he'd just missed something.

'I think we'd better go and see if your mummy is ready for us,' he said, scooping up the baby and heading for the stairs, dodging as she grabbed for his beard, catching her hands.

'No, you don't, miss.' She stuck out her bottom lip and he laughed. 'You're going to be a handful.'

His handful…

Then, catching a faint whiff of the faintest scent, he let go of her hands and didn't stop her when she grabbed hold of his ear, distracted by a familiar combination of soap, shampoo, something more that was uniquely Grace, and he knew exactly what had disturbed him.

It was this scent that had always been the first thing to greet him when he'd unlocked the basement door and walked in, usually at some unearthly hour in the morning after a non-stop flight from Sydney.

It was on the sheets when he'd stretched out to sleep, but had instead lain awake, imagining her leaning over to pull them tight, tuck them in, smooth the pillowcases into place.

Leaning over him, her long hair trailing over his skin, the scent of her shampoo—everything about her so familiar and yet completely new.

It had been so real that he had almost fooled himself that this time it would be all right, almost believed that this time she would look at him and the intervening years would be wiped out.

Instead, when he saw her, he'd get a quick, surprised smile as if his arrival was the last thing on her mind and he'd know that she hadn't given him a single thought since the last time he had been home. An impression confirmed when she'd appear at dinner with some decent, straightforward man in tow. A man who'd get the real smile. And he'd be certain that this time she'd found what she was looking for. Not him. Never him.

And he'd tell himself that he'd always known this was how it would be. Tell himself that it was right, that he was glad for her because he was the last man on earth she needed in her life.

Tell himself that he'd imagined the scent.

But he hadn't imagined the scent on his sheets, his pillows. She'd been there time after time in his basement flat, preparing things for his arrival, just as she'd been there a minute ago, watching him with Posie.

As he walked into the kitchen she turned from the stove where, apron wrapped around her, she was laying strips of bacon in a pan as casually as if it were the only thing on her mind.

'I thought you'd be hungry,' she said brightly enough and, if he hadn't known that a minute earlier she'd been down in the basement, he might have been fooled.

'Why didn't you say something?' he challenged. 'When you came downstairs.'

'Peekaboo?' she offered, not looking at him.

'That would have done.'

'You two were having such a good time I didn't want to butt in and spoil your game.'

'Three wouldn't have been a crowd.'

'Peekaboo is a game for two.' She half turned. 'What gave me away?'

'Your scent.'

She frowned. 'I'm not wearing any scent.'

Posie, tired from her games, was falling asleep against his shoulder and he gently lowered her into her crib, held his breath as her eyes flew open, felt something inside him melt as they slowly drifted shut. Awake, playing, she'd been a bundle of energy, but lying asleep he could see just how fragile, how vulnerable she was. Being a parent wasn't just a full-time job, it was a twenty-four/seven responsibility. There was no time off. No putting the job first.

Phoebe hadn't worked since the day she had married Michael. With two tricky teenagers and a large house to run, she hadn't had time. Grace was different. She had her own business, small by his standards, but it had taken years of hard work to build it up from that first market stall and it was her life. Had been her life. Now there was Posie and she couldn't do it on her own. Maybe she wouldn't get that chance.

He'd tried to lay it out in words of one syllable, warn her what might happen, but he knew he could never let anyone take Posie from her mother. His mother could be bought. His father worked in a politically sensitive environment and he wouldn't want his personal life plastered over the tabloids. But that wasn't the end of it. Grace was going to need help, support. And Posie would need a father. Not just a reluctant sperm donation, but someone like Michael.

He felt his chest tighten painfully.

Not him.

He wasn't like Michael. He didn't take in strays. Wasn't a nest-builder. His apartment had been decorated by a professional, looked like a show house rather than a home. He still had worlds to conquer. She needed someone like Toby Makepeace…

He looked up and realised that while he'd been thinking about her, she'd been watching him standing over the baby. She wasn't exactly smiling, but there was a softness about her eyes, her mouth…

He straightened. 'No scent?' he said, stepping back from the abyss yawning at his feet.

'None,' she said, turning away to lift a basket of eggs from a hook.

'I beg to differ,' he said.

'Oh?' She looked over her shoulder at him. 'And just how are you going to prove it, Josh Kingsley?'

He joined her at the Aga. 'Like this,' he said, bending to her hair, the feathery wisps tickling as he breathed in the scent of her shampoo.

'All you'll smell if you stand there is bacon,' she said, twitching away.

'You're using one of those herbal shampoos,' he said.

'Me and the rest of the world.'

'No…' This wasn't something mass-produced. It came from some little specialist shop; it was a national chain now, but it had started in Maybridge and Phoebe had been a fan. 'Rosemary?'

She said something that sounded like, 'Humph.'

As she made a move to escape him, he put his hands on her shoulders and kept her where she was while he lowered his head to lay his cheek against the smooth, fair skin of her neck.

She twitched at the touch of his beard, trembled beneath his hands just as she had when, eighteen years old, she'd come to him. When they'd made love….

'Lemon and myrtle,' she said abruptly. 'From Amaryllis Jones in the craft centre.'

That was it.

The scent on his sheets. The thought acted like an aphrodisiac and he backed off before he embarrassed them both.

'I had the lemon,' he said. 'I'd never have got the myrtle. What is that?'

'A bush. Small white flowers, long stamens, lovely scent. There's one in the garden,' she said, picking up a fish slice and holding it up like an offensive weapon. 'If you'd rather shower first, I can put this on hold.'

A cold shower might be a good idea. But he couldn't quite bring himself to leave her.

He'd dreamed about Grace. Hot, sexy dreams that left him aching with need, but he'd never responded to her physical presence with such an instant hard-on before. Not since the night when, trembling in his arms, she'd kissed him and he'd lost his mind.

But then, since that first night, she'd held him off with all the force of a quarterback scenting a touchdown.

'I'll eat first,' he said, pulling out a chair, sitting down, watching her as she fussed with the breakfast, avoiding eye contact, flustered in a way he'd never seen her before. But then she'd always had someone on hand to run interference for her when he'd been home. All those good, steady men. Never the same one twice… 'So,' he said, 'what game can the two of us play with Posie?'

The fish slice slipped from her fingers and clattered on the quarry tiles.

'I thought I might walk into town,' she said, picking it up, rinsing it under the tap, drying it. 'Posie and I could do with some fresh air. You could take my van if you like.' Then, when he didn't say anything—since not saying anything was prompting her mouth to run away with her—she pulled a face. 'Maybe not. It doesn't quite fit the tycoon image, does it? Phoebe's car is in the garage.' He saw her eyes dim as she thought about her sister. Tried to imagine what this last week had been like for her. 'Eggs?' she asked. 'One, two?'

'Just one, thanks. I'll walk in with you and Posie, Grace. I seem to have spent the last three days sitting in a plane and I need to stretch my legs.'

Grace, who he'd seen handle the tiniest beads with the precision of a surgeon, missed the edge of the pan and, as the egg shattered against the hotplate, sizzling and burning, she leapt back with a tiny scream.

'Did you burn yourself?'

He was with her before she could answer, taking her hand, turning it over to see what damage she'd done. Leading her to the sink to run it under the cold tap.

She shook her head, not looking at him but back at the stove. 'It's nothing, just a splash. I need to clean up…'

'I'll do it,' he said, leaving her with the utmost reluctance, but knowing that, if he didn't, she'd do it herself. He removed the pan with the bacon from the hotplate and picking up the slice that was having a very hard day, used it to scrape burnt egg off the cooker.

She turned off the tap.

'Grace…'

'It's fine. Nothing. There's so much to do.' She pushed long slender fingers, which could conjure up an original piece of jewellery out of nothing, through her short hair. 'I need to go and make up a bed for your mother. Did you say she's coming this morning? Someone will have to be here to let her in. Maybe I'd better stay. She'll want to see Posie, too. I asked one of my friends to take care of her on the day of the funeral. I thought she'd stay on for a while…'

He saw her stop, think about that and then, as she remembered what he'd said about her being at the back of the queue when it came to Posie's future, turn to him for reassurance.

Thinking that if she hadn't stayed, couldn't spare the time to wait and see her baby granddaughter, there was no possibility that she'd be interested in custody.

He would not give her that. Could not. Not until he knew whether Michael had made a new will. If he had, then he would surely have named Grace as her guardian. If not, it would be open season…

'I have no idea what my mother will do about Posie, Grace. But you can be certain that, whatever it is, it will be for her own benefit rather than as a result of grandmotherly instincts belatedly kicking in.'

He wanted her to understand that she was going to have

to fight to hold on to her baby. His parents, her mother, maybe even him.

She stared at him. 'You really do hate her, don't you? Your mother.'

'No,' he said, grabbing the kitchen roll to wipe the surface of the Aga. 'I don't hate her.'

For a long time he'd thought he did but he'd learned, over the years, that relationships were never that simple. He'd come to understand that people were driven by desires, forces beyond their control.

Maybe that was the dominant trait that both he and Michael had inherited—the selfish gene that allowed them to fix on a goal without thought for the havoc created in the wake of achievement.

His father had left them both for a younger woman and, in her misery, his mother had jettisoned him to chase her own second chance of happiness.

Much in the same way that, justifying himself that it was in her best interests, he'd walked away from Grace. Had pursued and married the girl every other man he knew had wanted to bed, without a thought what marriage to him would be like. Alone for weeks on end. Not anger, no sense of betrayal, only relief when she'd found someone to console her…

Then, realising that Grace was still watching him, trying to read his expression, he said, 'If I could have hated her, it wouldn't have hurt so much when she left.' Facing a truth he'd fought since she'd left him with Michael. Sharing it with Grace because she was the one person he knew would understand.

'I tried to hate my mother, too,' she said. 'Hate is so much easier. But the bad stuff is mixed up with all kinds of good memories.'

'What good memories?' he asked. She had never talked about her life with her crazy hippie mother, her life on the road, and he'd never pushed her, even in teasing, instinctively knowing that it was beyond painful. 'What good memories?' he repeated.

Grace thought about it as Josh returned the bacon to the hotplate, cracked an egg into the pan and dropped a couple of slices of bread in the toaster.

'Stringing beads is my first stand-out memory,' she said. 'My mother was making jewellery to sell at a craft fair and, to keep me from bothering her, she gave me a thin piece of leather and a box of big bright beads so that I could make my own necklace.'

She remembered sitting at a table in the old minibus they were living in, sorting through the box of painted wooden beads, totally absorbed by the smooth feel of them, the different sizes, vivid colours. Laying them out in rows until she found a combination of colours and sizes that pleased her. Her delight as each shiny bead slid down the dark leather and the vision in her head became real.

Best of all, she remembered her mother's smile of approval.

'I bet you still have it somewhere,' Josh said, bringing her back to the present.

'No.' She grabbed the toast as it popped up, put it on a plate, reached for a clean slice and flipped the egg over. 'Someone saw me wearing it at the craft fair and asked my mother if she had another one like it.'

'Absolutely not,' he said, smiling at her. 'It was a Grace McAllister original. Your first.'

'Absolutely. My fate was sealed with that first sale.'

'Sale?' His smile faded as he realised what she was saying. 'Are you telling me that your mother sold the necklace you'd made for yourself?' Shocked didn't cover it. 'That's a good memory?'

'Of course. I'd made something someone liked enough to pay for,' she said, glancing up at him. 'That made me feel special. I bet you didn't feel a bigger thrill when you signed your first contract, Josh. And I made myself another one when I got home.'

'She still shouldn't have done it.' He made no attempt to

disguise his disgust. 'If that is as good as it got, I dread to think what the bad stuff was like.'

There were the times they'd been hungry, cold, but she and her mother had cuddled up together—they weren't the bad times. Bad wasn't her mother. It was other people…

'Bad was angry people. Shouting, forcing us to move on in the middle of the night.' She stared at the bacon sizzling in the heavy-bottomed, expensive pan standing on the Aga. The kind of luxury that she took for granted these days. 'Bad is never knowing where you're going to be when you wake up. Another new school where the kids call you filthy names because you live in a camper van parked on the land of someone who wants you gone. Seeing your mother dragged off by the police, arrested, just because she lashed out at someone who'd smashed the windscreen of her home. Running into the woods to hide so that the police wouldn't take you away, put you into care…'

She stopped. Where had all that come from? All those long-buried memories. Things she'd hadn't thought about in a long time. A world she'd left behind on the day Phoebe and Michael had picked her up from Social Services, brought her home. On the day that Josh had tossed her his spare crash helmet and taken her into school on the back of his motorbike.

Memories that she'd almost blotted from her mind. Apart from that apparently everlasting residual fear, the one about waking up and not knowing where she was. The one that still had the power to give her nightmares. That still brought her out in a cold sweat when she had to spend a night away at a craft fair….

Then, having apparently rendered him speechless, she said, 'There's juice in the fridge, Josh. Help yourself.'

'Why didn't you tell me?' he asked, pouring juice into a couple of glasses she'd put on the table, bringing one over to her. 'I knew your mother was a "traveller", that she'd got into a bit of bother with the law. That Phoebe rescued you from care and was granted a Parental Responsibility Order so that your mother couldn't take you back on the road. But not the rest.'

When she didn't answer, he looked up.

'I thought we were friends, Grace.'

Were. Past tense. Because once you'd spent the night naked with a man, utterly exposed, all barriers down, it could never be that simple ever again.

'Are you saying that you told me everything?' she said flippantly. 'I don't think so.'

'Everything that mattered. Do you think I talked to anyone else about my parents the way I talked to you?'

She knew exactly how much his father's desertion had hurt him. What it had done to him when, six months later, his mother had flown off to the other side of the world with someone new.

He'd put on a couldn't-care-less face for the rest of the world but, a few weeks after she'd moved in, when life was suddenly unbelievably wonderful, she'd rushed into the garden with a letter that had arrived for him from Japan. Thrilled by the strangeness of it.

He'd taken it from her, glanced at it and then, without bothering to open it, he'd torn it in two, then torn it again and again before finally discarding it, letting the breeze take the pieces, the savagery of it shocking her into a little scream.

'It was from my mother,' he said, as if that explained everything. Then, 'Sorry. Did you want the stamps?'

The line had been a study in throwaway carelessness, but a shake in his voice had betrayed him, as had a suspicion of brightness in his eyes that she'd recognised only too well. And she'd put her thin arms around him and hugged him while he cried.

This was the first time either of them had ever referred to that moment and their eyes connected as they remembered, relived that moment of anguish when he'd been more completely hers than even at the moment of sexual release.

'So?' he said. 'Why didn't you tell me how it was?'

'Fear.' Faced with the disaster of the last week, the deceit, how could she be anything but honest with him?

'Fear?'

Fear that if he knew, he'd look at her the same way those other kids had.

Not that honest…

'I was afraid that if people found out about me, they'd be angry that I was living here. That I'd be forced to leave. And Phoebe, too.'

'But that's ridiculous.'

His response was natural. How could he possibly know how savage people could be when they felt threatened by those who didn't conform to the rules they lived by, who chose to live a different way?

'I know that now. Michael loved Phoebe too much, was too big a man to have buckled under disapproval, peer pressure.'

But she had often wondered what Michael's parents had thought of his wife. While her own mother had been accepted, welcomed on her rare visits, neither of his parents had ever been to this house while Phoebe was alive. And there had been no attempt to reconcile Josh with his parents, something that would normally have been a priority for Michael. He'd never talked about them. Had dismissed without consideration her tentative suggestion that he invite them to Posie's christening. There had to have been more to that than just a messy break-up and divorce.

'Back then,' she said, 'I didn't know, didn't understand how special your brother was.'

'I don't suppose anyone does until it's too late to tell them.' He looked across at Posie, sleeping peacefully in her crib, and said, 'It's going to be up to us, isn't it?'

'Us?' She took a sip of the juice, put the glass down, reached up for a plate.

'To make sure that Posie only has good memories.'

'Oh, right. And how exactly do you intend to do that, Josh? Are you planning to phone them in from whatever exotic location you're in at the time? Tell her about the great beaches, the palm trees?' Then, 'Or maybe send her postcards? That would certainly give her a head start on a stamp collection…'

She stopped. Swallowed. She'd spoken without thinking but he'd think she'd mentioned the stamps deliberately. 'I'm sorry. I—'

'Maybe I should take her back to Australia with me,' he cut in, stopping her apology in its tracks. 'So that she can experience them for herself. It's a great place for kids to grow up.'

Her grip tightened on the handle of the slice but she refused to be rattled.

'The best place for a child is to be with people who love her enough to put her needs first,' she said, keeping her back to him. 'Who'd look after her in Australia when you're off conquering new worlds?'

'You?'

Now he had her attention and she swung round to face him. 'Excuse me, but are you offering me a job as my own daughter's nanny?'

Maybe it was just as well that the doorbell saved him from answering because this was a conversation going downhill fast.

'Your breakfast is burned,' she said coldly, handing him the slice and, leaving him to take it from the pan or not as he pleased, went to answer the door.

The slender woman standing on the doorstep was swathed in bright silk, jewellery dripping from every possible location. As exotic as any bird of paradise.

'Mum…?'

She didn't reply, just dropped the bag she was carrying, stepped forward and wrapped her arms around her, cloaking her in the faint aroma of some exotic spicy fragrance. For the first time in a very long time Grace did not resist or pull back as soon as she could. Right now she needed her mother in ways she barely understood and they clung together for a long time, not needing to speak.

It was, finally, her mother who drew back first, her gaze fixed on something behind her, and Grace didn't need to turn around to know that Josh had followed her into the hall.

'Hello, Dawn.'

'Josh…' she said, acknowledging him, but her eyes were on the baby he was holding with a possessiveness that made Grace's blood run cold. 'Hello, my sweetheart,' she said, holding out her arms. 'Come to your grandma.'

For a moment Grace thought Josh wasn't going to surrender her, but Posie, attracted by the bright colours, was smiling at this interesting new arrival and, after what felt like the longest hesitation in history, he gave her up.

'I'm going to take that shower, Grace,' he said. 'If you can be ready to leave by half past eight?' Then, 'You do still want to come into town? Dawn can let my mother in if she arrives while we're out.'

She had never wanted to go into town, but she couldn't put it off any longer. And they had unfinished business to discuss that she didn't want anyone else overhearing.

'Will you be all right, Mum? I had a commission for a tiara that has to be delivered by the end of the week.' Then, straightening for a fight she hadn't anticipated but would not duck, 'And you're right about the workshop, Josh. It's my livelihood and I need to make arrangements to keep it ticking over while I think about how I can fit it around Posie's needs.'

That brought something that could almost have been interpreted as a smile to his lips as he recognised the challenge. 'You're not interested in hearing my offer, then?'

'Posie and I are happy here.' And, before he could say any more, 'We'll be ready to leave at half past eight.'

Neither her mother nor Grace spoke until they heard the basement door shut, at which point they let go of the breath they'd been collectively holding.

'That man is so intense,' her mother said. 'Not a bit like his poor brother.'

'No. But they were very close.'

'Were they?' She turned to the infant in her arms and they inspected one another, her mother with a searching look, Posie with her little forehead wrinkled in a frown. 'What offer did Josh Kingsley make you, Grace?'

'He didn't make an offer.' Well, he hadn't. She'd cut him off before he'd said the words. 'It was just a joke.'

'Really? He didn't look as if he was joking. Only I did wonder, if he's been appointed guardian, whether he'll want to take Posie back to Australia with him.'

'He can't do that.'

'Oh?' she said. 'Are you quite sure about that? She's a beautiful child and he seems…attached.'

'He wouldn't. He's never in one place for more than a week and children need stability. Order. He knows that.' They both knew that.

'They are important,' her mother agreed, 'but knowing that they're loved is what really counts.' Then, looking at her granddaughter, 'Phoebe must have been so happy. I'm glad she had these few weeks when her world was complete.'

'Yes…' Grace tried to say more, but there was just a great big lump in her throat.

'And you, Grace? What will make your world complete?'

She shook her head. Some things were never meant to be.

'Come on through to the kitchen. I'll get you something to eat,' she said, anxious to change the subject.

'I'm not hungry, just tired.' Then, 'I'm sorry I didn't get here in time to share the burden, help with the arrangements.'

Grace shook her head. 'They'd left instructions. They chose a woodland burial site. It's very peaceful. I'll take you there when you've recovered. Josh hasn't seen it, either. He only arrived yesterday.'

Her mother nodded. 'I need to make a phone call, let someone know I've arrived. Then perhaps a bath and a nap?'

'Why don't you use my flat? I'm staying down here with

Posie so you'll be quiet up there,' she said, picking up her mother's bag and heading for the stairs. 'Private,' she added, wondering quite how Josh's mother would react when they met.

'Nice idea, but I'm not sure that I could cope with all those stairs.' She pulled a face. 'Years of damp and cold, living in vans, hasn't done my hips any favours.'

Concerned, Grace stopped. 'Are you okay? I could sort you out something on the ground floor for sleeping, but there isn't a shower on this floor.'

'I'm going to need replacement joints sooner rather than later but I can just about cope with one flight. I'd like to make my call before I go up, though. I need to tell a friend that I arrived safely.'

That was such an unexpected thing for her free-as-a-bird mother to say that Grace said, 'A friend?' Then, 'You've met someone?'

'You think I'm too old?'

'No, Mum. I'm just jealous.' Then, 'Help yourself to the phone in Michael's study. I'll put your bag in the front bedroom on the right—it's the one nearest to the stairs. Then I'll get Posie ready for her outing.'

'You're taking her with you?' She sounded disappointed. 'I would have taken care of her.'

'You need a rest and, to be honest, we could both do with some fresh air. I thought we'd come home through the park so that she can feed the ducks. You know how Phoebe loved to do that.'

Her mother laughed. 'Phoebe?'

'Wasn't it Phoebe who once gave all the bread we had to the greedy little beasts?'

'No. She gave the bread to you and you gave it to the ducks.'

'Are you sure?'

'Oh, yes. She was supposed to be looking after you so that I could put together some stuff to sell at a craft market.'

Grace had vivid memories of her mother bent over a table,

working long into the night to put together her intricate necklaces and bracelets. Easy in hindsight to understand how hard it must have been for her, a single mother trying to make enough money to keep her girls fed and clothed as she lived the travelling lifestyle that she'd taken to with the man she'd loved. Had never left, even when he'd disappeared one day. How lonely it must have been.

A scenario that she was now faced with. Not that Posie would ever be hungry or afraid. Not while she had breath in her body.

'Leaving us all without supper was her way of letting me know that she had much more interesting things to do than babysit her little sister.'

'No!' Grace found that hard to believe. 'Phoebe was always so protective. So caring.' So...*good*. Or was that the grown-up Phoebe she was thinking of?

'It was me she had a problem with, Grace. Not you. We both know that I would never have made the shortlist for greatest mother in the world. Something she made very clear when I came to fetch you after my twenty-eight days for vandalism and disturbing the peace.'

'You came for me?' Her mother hadn't just abandoned her, taken the easy option, the get-out-of-jail-free card? 'I never knew.'

Phoebe had never told her. It seemed that her big sister was better at keeping secrets than she'd ever imagined.

'We agreed that it was for the best. You didn't have her rebelliousness, her toughness. You needed to feel safe. I loved you more than words could say and it was like cutting off my right arm to leave you, but I knew you'd be happier with her. That it would be easier for you if you weren't torn by any foolish loyalty to me.' She kissed Posie's downy head and handed her over. 'She would have been such a wonderful mother. But you will be, too. Much better than I ever was.'

There was such a world of need in her eyes that Grace put an arm around her, held her and said, 'You gave me up because you loved me. That's the hardest, finest thing for a mother to do.'

'Oh…' There were tears in her eyes as she pushed her away, saying, 'Go and pretty yourselves up. I've got a call to make.'

CHAPTER SIX

DRESSING Posie, putting together everything she'd need for the morning, took nearly all the time Grace had so that 'prettying herself up' consisted of little more than pulling a comb through her short hair.

Then she fastened jade button earrings to her lobes and a matching necklace of overlapping disks of the same stone around her throat. Make-up she could live without, but jewellery was her business and she'd never been anywhere since she'd been a toddler without something fancy around her neck or wrist—her 'sparklies'—and she'd feel naked without them.

She settled the necklace into place, trying not to think about Josh, his hands on her shoulders as he'd leaned into her neck to hunt down some elusive scent. The feel of his beard brushing against her skin, sending gooseflesh shivering through her.

The last time they'd been that close, that intimate, they'd been naked. This morning, when she'd felt the warmth of his breath against her ear, been swamped by the scent of a man still warm from his bed, she'd wanted to be naked again.

She slipped on her suit jacket, buttoned it up and, without bothering to check her reflection, fetched Posie from the nursery and went downstairs.

Josh looked up, said nothing, as she hurried into the kitchen ten minutes later than she'd promised. He just looked at her and she was convinced he could see every hot, wicked thought that had been running through her mind, distracting her, slowing her down.

'Ready?' she asked.

Stupid question. He was showered, wearing faded jeans and a soft suede jacket that emphasized the width of his shoulders and brought out the amber flecks in his grey eyes. He had obviously been there for some time since all trace of the breakfast disaster had been removed and he was sitting at the table, looking through the local paper.

He closed it, got up and said, 'Can I do anything?'

'G-get the buggy? It's in the mud room,' she said, opening the fridge, fitting a bottle into its own special little cold box, slipping it into the carrier that contained all Posie's essentials, exactly as she'd seen Phoebe do dozens of times. Keeping her hands behind her back to hide fingers itching to help.

What she wouldn't have given for that yearning now. To see Michael instead of Josh setting up the buggy, take Posie and fasten her into the little pink nest. Put the carrier in the rack beneath it.

'Not bad,' she said. 'For a first effort.'

He didn't answer but took the handle of the buggy, wheeled it into the hall.

The steps weren't exactly easy to navigate, as she knew from experience, and, having opened the door, she made a move to help. Unnecessary. Josh just lifted the buggy, with Posie and all her belongings in it, and carried them down the steps as if it weighed no more than a feather.

A nice trick if you could manage it, she thought and, since possession was nine-tenths of the law, by the time she'd shut the door and reached the footpath he was already walking away from her, forcing her to trot to catch up.

'Slow down,' she said crossly. 'This isn't a race.'

Without taking his hand off the buggy, he lifted his elbow

and, glancing down at her, said, 'Hang on. You can slow me down if I'm speeding.'

He wanted her to put her arm through his? Walk along arm in arm as if they were Michael and Phoebe…?

As if they were a couple. Lovers…

She swallowed, imagining her hand against the soft suede, her fingers resting on the hard sinewy flesh beneath it. She wanted that closeness in a way that was beyond imagining. Wanted it too much to be able to risk it.

'You're all right,' she said.

He didn't argue, simply stopped, took her hand and placed it under his arm. 'Whatever happens, you're not on your own, Grace,' he said, then, without giving her time to resist, to object, he continued, rather more slowly, on his way.

The suede was as soft to the touch as a baby's breath, while beneath it the familiar muscular arm seemed to burn through to her fingers, setting light to the memory of him standing in the kitchen, naked to the waist, in the early light.

As a girl she'd clung to his waist when she'd ridden behind him on his bike, pressed to his back, sheltered from the force of the wind by his body. That had been a secret thrill, one that had given her more of a rush than the speed at which they had been flying along. One that Josh hadn't ever known about.

This was different. This closeness was not some careless thing, just part of being on the back of a motorbike. He'd made a deliberate choice, just as he had on her first day at school when he'd tossed her his spare helmet. As he paused, turned to cross the road, and his sleeve brushed against her cheek it was like the sun coming out. She wanted to lean into it, suck up that protective warmth.

All illusion. This was not his world. In a week, two at the most, he'd be gone, chasing endless horizons. That was fact. He'd be somewhere out of reach and she'd be alone.

And, with that thought, the true finality of what had happened crystallised in her mind. Until now she'd been skimming along, keeping the wheels ticking over, taking care of Posie. Coping with the details. Standing numbly in the church through hymns and eulogies. Even watching her sister and her husband being lowered into the dark earth, it hadn't seemed real.

Each morning, her first reaction was that momentary panic at waking in an unfamiliar room, the remembering that she was in the guest room next to the nursery because her sister was away for the weekend.

Only after that came the sickening moment when she remembered that Phoebe was never coming home again. But then Posie claimed her attention and there was no time for anything but the essentials. Laundry, feeding, bathing her, changing her. She was a full-time job all by herself.

Now, walking with Josh in Michael and Phoebe's place, an icy hand gripped at her stomach, her heart. This wasn't just for a few days. This was her life. There was only her to be responsible, make decisions, make sure that this precious baby…little girl…teenager…had the best life that she could give her.

'Grace?'

Josh stopped as she pulled away, gasping for breath, and, ignoring her as she took her hand off his arm, as she tried to keep him away, he let go of the buggy and, catching her by the shoulders, pulled her against him.

'They're gone, Josh,' she said, looking up, wanting him to see, to understand. 'They're never coming back.'

His only response was to wrap his arms tightly around her, press his cheek, his lips against her hair as if he could somehow keep out the world.

'Hush… It's all right.'

All right…

All right!

'How can anything be all right ever again?' She pulled back, flinging up her arms to push him away. 'It needs more than a hug and words to fix this, Josh. It isn't just us, there's a baby involved, one that you and I made, and we're responsible.' She knew she was making a scene, that people on their way into town were turning to look, but she didn't care. She had to make him see. 'It's not just for this week, or next week, but for *ever*. We're not just spectators in Posie's life, we're her—'

Josh grabbed her by the arm and pulled her, pushed Posie off the street and into the quiet of the park.

'—parents.'

Except it wasn't 'we'. It was her.

Or was it? Josh had said he had gone through Michael's papers last night. What had he found? What had made him warn her that she was bottom of the heap?

'Do you know what guardianship arrangements Michael made for Posie?' Because a man who'd taken time to plan his own funeral to make things easy for whoever was left to pick of pieces in the event of his death wouldn't leave something really important like that to chance. 'Stupid question. Of *course* you know. You're his executor. Even when you weren't talking to him, Michael still told you everything.'

'I can't tell you anything until I've spoken to Michael's lawyers.'

He let go of her arm, leaving a cold empty space, but that was what he always did. Went away. University, gap year, for ever. He leaned forward over the buggy, tenderly tucking the blanket around Posie where she'd kicked it loose in her sleep, then began to move on through the park.

'Can't? Or won't?' she demanded, planting her feet, refusing to take another step until he gave her an answer. 'What is it you're keeping from me?'

He stopped. 'It won't help.'

'I think I'm the best judge of what helps me, Josh.'

He glanced at her. 'You're wrong about Michael telling me everything. He didn't share whatever decision he'd made with me, which suggests there were unresolved issues.'

'I think we can both guess what they were.'

He shrugged. 'Maybe. There was some correspondence with his lawyer regarding the surrogacy and it's clear that Michael and Phoebe intended to draw up new wills once Posie was legally theirs, but as far as I can tell nothing had been signed.'

'So that means…?' She lifted her shoulders.

'I won't know for sure until I've talked to the lawyer. Even a draft setting out their wishes would be something.' He stretched out a hand. 'Come on. The sooner I get there, the sooner we'll both know where we stand.'

He didn't move to take her hand as he had before. This time he waited for her to choose, to meet him halfway. And, ignoring his hand, she tucked her own back under his arm. A gesture of trust.

'Maybe I should come with you.'

'You can trust me, Grace. I'll look after your interests. You'll be better occupied at the craft centre.'

'But…'

'As soon as I'm done, I'll join you. Once we know what we're faced with, we can talk it through. Make decisions.'

It made sense, she supposed. Then, as another thought struck her, 'Will you tell him? About Posie? About…' She swallowed. There was something so intimate about the fact that they'd created a baby together—even though they had been at opposite ends of the earth when it had happened—that she couldn't quite bring herself to say the words. Couldn't bring herself to say *us*.

'About our involvement in Posie's conception?' he filled in for her.

Involvement.

Good word. If you wanted to eradicate any suggestion of intimacy. And why not? There had only been one night of us and while for her it had been the only night, he had been the only one, she had no illusions that he'd spent the last ten years dreaming of her. That dream had been shattered the day he'd turned up with a beautiful young woman and announced they'd stopped over in Bali on their way to England and got married.

'That would be the involvement you just announced to a street full of people?'

Her hand flew to her mouth. 'I didn't!'

'I'm paraphrasing, but "…there's a baby that you and I made…" just about covers it.'

She groaned.

'Relax. Most people just wanted to get away from the mad woman as fast as they could.'

'You're just saying that to make me feel better.'

'No. I swear. At least three people crossed the street.'

'Only three?' She shook her head, but she was smiling.

'That's better. And, to answer your question, I don't think there's anything to be gained by telling him about us and robbing Phoebe and Michael of something they'd longed for with such a passion. It's nobody's business but ours, Grace.'

Ours. Us.

Josh savoured the words, drinking them in like a man who'd been wandering in the desert.

He'd locked himself out of Grace's life a long time ago. He hadn't fully understood why she'd been trapped like a fledgling, too scared to fly the nest that Phoebe and Michael had made for her. He'd accepted that it was somehow mixed up with her childhood, but he'd never pushed her to explain. Maybe he hadn't wanted to, preferring to tell himself that it was for the best, that she'd have slowed him down, instead of being honest with himself. Facing his own demons.

But those two tiny words—*ours, us*—like the infant who'd dropped off to sleep in the buggy, joined them in a unique alliance that set them apart from the rest of the world. They were a family.

He was a father and that was a responsibility he couldn't run away from.

They reached the corner where their ways divided but, instead of parting, they stood, her hand linking them together, and for a moment it seemed that she was as reluctant as him to break the connection.

He was on the point of suggesting that perhaps, after all, she should go with him to talk to Michael's lawyer, when she finally took her arm from his and said, 'I'd better let you go.'

He caught her hand. 'We're in this together, Grace.'

'Are we?'

'I'll do whatever it takes to protect Phoebe and Michael. I owe them that.'

'And Posie?'

'I'll protect her with my life.'

As he would Grace. He couldn't begin to guess how hard this was going to be for her. Desperate with worry about the future of a child who she had never, whether she'd admit it or not, truly given up, when she should be left in peace to grieve for her sister.

'This is all my fault,' she said. 'If I hadn't—'

'Don't!' He'd done everything he could to prevent her from having this baby, prevent himself from becoming a father, but he couldn't bear to hear her put what he'd wished into words. Not now he'd held Posie, seen her smile. 'Please, don't do that to yourself.'

Or to him.

She lifted her stricken face.

'But it's true. I wanted them to go away for the weekend, planned it, gave it to them as my treat because I wanted to have Posie to myself. Just for the weekend. Only for the weekend…'

Oh, dear God. It wasn't colluding with Phoebe that was tormenting her. She was blaming herself for the accident.

'No,' he said. And, when she would have argued, he said it again. 'No. It's always like this when someone dies,' he said. 'The guilt kicks in. You can only think of the things you did wrong. Or didn't do at all,' he added, thinking of his own miserable, selfish response to something that had made his brother so happy. 'They can overwhelm you, take on an importance completely out of proportion to their true meaning.'

She shook her head.

'You have to remember the good things. Remember how happy you made them both.' He squeezed her arm reassuringly, then touched the sleeping baby's head. 'I'll see you both later,' he said, taking a step back, saving the picture of the two of them in his mind before tearing himself away.

Grace unlocked the door to her workshop, kicking aside the mail so that she could get the buggy in, turning on the lights.

She'd expanded from her original tiny workroom, moving into this wonderful airy space when it had become vacant a couple of years ago.

She'd kept the walls and furnishings a stark black and white to accentuate the vivid colours of her jewellery. At one end there was a secure walk-in storage space for the basic tools of her trade and a tiny office. There was her working area, with her drawing board and the workbench where she put together her designs.

The centre of the room offered a display area for photographs of some of the special pieces she'd made, as well as the dramatic spiral stands that Toby had designed and made to display examples of her work.

There was a comfortable seating area for clients who came to discuss special commissions and at the far end was another long workbench where she worked with the students who took her classes.

She didn't waste time going through the mail, but put it to one side to take home with her. Instead, she made the most of the fact that Posie was asleep to download and pack up the Internet orders for beads, findings, the jewellery kits that kept the cash flow ticking over.

After that she called Abby, a stay-at-home mum who'd

taken one of her classes and proved to be one of her most talented students. She was happy to come in for a few hours a day for the next couple of weeks and, while Grace was waiting for her to arrive so that she could walk her through the Web site ordering systems, she took the armature for the tiara she'd designed from the workroom, the tray with the teardrop pearls and each size and colour of semi-precious stone she would use, counted and placed in individual compartments. Then, with the deceptively simple design in front of her, she began to build the sparkling fairy tale confection that a young bride would wear on the most special day of her life.

When, finally, it was finished, she sat back and looked at it, glad she'd come here. Glad she'd done something positive. Something life-affirming.

Posie, who'd been an angel and had slept while she'd worked, finally woke and began to make her presence felt.

'Well, haven't you been a good baby,' she said, as she lifted her bag from the carrier and plugged in her bottle-warmer before changing her.

She was just about to settle on the sofa in the customer area, when there was a tap at the door.

Josh would have just walked in despite the 'closed' sign on the door and, expecting it to be Abby, she called out, 'It's open.' Then, as she realised it was neither, she said, 'Oh, Toby…'

Her disappointment must have been evident because he didn't come beyond the doorway.

'I know you're not open but I saw your light on and I thought I'd come over and see if there was anything you need. If it's a bad time…'

Toby Makepeace restored and made bespoke rocking horses across the cobbled yard of what had once been a huge coaching inn, but had long since been converted into craft workshops and small boutiques. He was easy to get along with and she'd taken him home as her 'date' the last time Josh had come home on a proper visit.

Still trying to prove to him, or maybe just to herself, that he didn't mean anything to her. No, definitely to herself. He hadn't given her a thought a minute after he'd left her sleeping in his bed.

Toby, unlike her other 'dates', had quickly cottoned on to the reason for his presence and had played his part to the hilt. Michael had teased her about him for weeks afterwards, referring to him as her 'lovelorn swain' until Phoebe had finally told him to stop embarrassing her.

Had Phoebe seen, understood more than she had ever let on? She had never said anything, but she'd never pressed her about boyfriends, either. She'd never remarked on the fact, that despite the fact that Grace had always said she was too busy to get involved, she had always managed to have a date when Josh had come home.

It must have been blindingly obvious, now she came to think about it. Bless Phoebe…

Toby had laughed when she had told him and it had somehow cemented a genuine friendship and he had been the first person she'd thought of when she'd needed help at the hospital.

'No,' she said, 'it's never a bad time to see a friend. I don't think I ever thanked you properly for what you did.'

'Don't even think about it,' Toby said, closing the door, coming across and giving her a hug. Leaving his hand on her arm. It was no more than a gesture of comfort from a friend, but it was where Josh's hand had so recently lain. It felt so much like an intrusion that it took all her concentration not to pull away. 'Anything I can do, you know you only have to ask.'

'Actually, I'm just about to feed Posie. If you really want to make yourself useful, you could put on a pot of coffee.'

Posie, growing impatient, began to whimper.

'Poor little angel,' Toby said, touching a finger lightly to her cheek before taking himself off to fill the coffee-maker. 'But at least she's still got her real mummy to take care of her.'

Grace sighed. There really was no point in explaining the

finer points of surrogacy. She supposed most people would think that. She'd thought it herself until Josh had put her straight. She glanced at her watch. It had been more than an hour since they'd gone their separate ways.

What on earth could be taking so long?

Nothing good, she was sure. But there was nothing she could do about it now and she crossed to the sofa, settled herself in the corner against the arm and offered Posie the bottle. She sucked for a moment, then pulled away.

'What's up, sweetpea? I thought you were hungry.' She offered her the bottle again and this time she seemed to settle.

'Do these need posting?' Toby said, distracting her.

'Sorry?'

'These packages,' he said, nodding towards the pile of padded envelopes on her desk as he spooned coffee in the filter. 'I'm going that way at lunch time. I'll drop them in at the post office if you like.'

'Oh, right. Yes. That would be a huge help,' she said, seizing on his offer. 'If you're sure.'

'I wouldn't offer if I didn't mean it.'

'You're a brick. Pass me my bag and I'll give you some money.' Then, 'They all need to be sent "signed for",' she apologised as she handed over the notes.

'No problem,' he said, tucking the money into his back pocket before sitting beside her. 'It'll mean all the more time to chat up that dark-haired girl behind the counter.'

'Sarah?' She smiled. 'Good choice. She's absolutely lovely. So how long has that been going on?'

He shrugged. 'I've been taking my post to her about twice a week since she started there.'

'And that would be what—five, six months?'

'I thought I'd take it slowly.'

'Er… No. That's not slow, Toby. That's pathetic. Why don't you just ask her out?'

'Because, if she said no, sheer embarrassment would mean

I'd have to go all the way into town to the main post office whenever I wanted a stamp.'

Grace clucked like a chicken and he laughed. 'I know, it's pathetic. But the main post office is a mile away.' Then, as Posie spat out the bottle again and began to grizzle, he said, 'What's the matter with her?'

'It's my fault. I usually wear something of Phoebe's when I feed her,' Grace replied. 'For the scent,' she explained. 'But I didn't think to bring anything with me.' She slipped a couple of buttons on her shirt. 'Maybe this will help. Phoebe used to hold her next to her skin.'

'As if she were breastfeeding?'

'What do you know about it?' she asked, laughing.

'I've got sisters,' he said. 'And sisters-in-law. Half a dozen of them. I've lost count of the number of nieces and nephews I have.'

'Right. Well, if I need any advice I'll know where to come,' she said, pushing aside her shirt a little and holding the baby close so that her cheek was against her skin. Drawn by the warmth, Posie immediately turned towards her and, after a moment or two, took the rubber teat of the feeder.

'That's so beautiful,' he said.

'Oh, Toby…'

And when, without warning, her eyes stung with tears that she could do nothing about, he put his arm around her, pulling her against his shoulder so that her tears soaked into his sleeve.

'I'm sorry,' she said. 'This is stupid.' She didn't even know what she was crying about. Phoebe and Michael. Posie. Josh…

Maybe all of them.

'It's okay,' he said. 'Go ahead. Let it out. It'll do you good.'

He still had his arm around her when the door opened and Josh walked in, coming to an abrupt halt at the sight of the three of them.

For a moment no one said anything, then Toby murmured,

just loud enough for him to hear, 'I'm sorry, Grace, I thought I'd locked the door.'

The shock on Josh's face at finding her with Toby's arm around her was very nearly as ridiculous as her own sense of guilt.

She had nothing to feel guilty about.

Toby was a friend—he'd been there when Josh had been communing with his guilt up a mountain.

But Josh was clearly reading something a lot more significant into the situation. And why wouldn't he, when she'd gone to such lengths to convince him that she was involved with the man?

But enough was enough and she pulled free of his arm, rubbing her palm across her wet cheek. 'Haven't you got an urgent date with the post office, Toby?' she reminded him before he completely forgot himself.

'You're going to throw me out before I have a cup of that fabulous coffee I've made for you?' he said, apparently determined to give Josh a reprise of his 'lovelorn swain' act.

'Abby will be here when you get back with the receipts,' she said, cutting him off before he could get going. 'Buy her a cake and I'm sure she'll take the hint. My treat.' Then, 'Buy two,' she said meaningfully.

'Two?'

'A red velvet cupcake is supposed to be irresistible,' she said.

'Got it,' he murmured, finally getting to his feet. Then, as he made a move, she put her hand on his arm, detaining him. 'Thanks for the shoulder.'

'Any time,' he said, covering her hand with his own, kissing her cheek, going for an Oscar. 'Anything.' Then, touching his finger to Posie's cheek. 'Bye, baby. Be good for Grace.'

Then, gathering the packages from her desk, he headed for the door, where Josh was blocking his way.

'Makepeace,' Josh said, his acknowledgement curt to the point of rudeness.

'Kingsley,' he responded mildly. 'I was sorry to hear about your brother. I liked him a lot.' The mildness was deceptive. If he'd actually said, *'Unlike you...'* he couldn't have made himself plainer. 'We missed you at his funeral.'

Josh said nothing, merely stepped aside to let him out, then closed the door after him and slipped the catch.

CHAPTER SEVEN

'I'M EXPECTING someone,' Grace protested.

'Whoever it is will knock,' Josh replied, crossing to the coffee pot. He turned over a couple of cups, opened the fridge. 'There's no milk. Shall I call back your gallant and ask him to bring you a carton?'

Gallant.

It was marginally better than 'lovelorn swain', she supposed. But only marginally.

'Don't bother for me,' she said, and he poured two cups of black coffee and placed them on the low table set in front of the sofa.

'You were a lot longer than I expected,' she said, glancing up at him as Posie spit out the teat, with a finality that suggested that any further attempt to persuade her to take any more would be a waste of time. 'What took you so long?'

'There was a lot to go through, but clearly I needn't have worried that you'd be lonely.'

Feeling trapped on the sofa, Grace got up, lifted the baby to her shoulder and, gently rubbing her back, began to pace.

'I didn't realise you and Toby Makepeace were still a hot item.'

Hot?

Hardly…

'When Toby saw the light, he came over to see if there was anything he could do, Josh. It's what friends do.'

'Yes, I got the "any time, anything" message. Including the shoulder to cry on,' he said, as she turned and came face to face with him. 'You'll forgive my surprise. I had assumed you were, momentarily, unattached.'

He invested 'momentarily' with more than its usual weight, bringing a flush to her wet cheeks, drawing quite unnecessary attention to them.

Josh produced a clean handkerchief and, taking her chin in his hand, he gently blotted first her eyes, then her cheeks, before unbuttoning one of the pockets on her thin silk shirt and tucking it against her breast.

She opened her mouth but no words came and she closed it again. Then jumped as he carefully refastened the buttons she had slipped open for Posie, her entire body trembling as the warmth of his fingers shot like an electric charge to her heart.

'Don't…' was all she could manage. 'Please.'

It was too painful. Too sweet…

He let his hands drop, stepping away from her, and it took all she had not to scream out a desperate, *No…*, because that felt wrong, too.

'In view of the fact that you were carrying a baby for Phoebe,' he continued calmly, as if nothing had happened. As if he hadn't just touched her, switching her on as easily as if he'd flipped a light switch, undoing, in a moment, ten years of keeping all her feelings battened down.

She stared at him, uncomprehending, having entirely lost the thread of what he was saying.

'I don't imagine there are many men who could handle that. Not even Toby Makepeace.'

Toby. The surrogacy…

Got it.

'Actually, you might be surprised. There are surrogates who, having completed their own families, want to help childless couples achieve their own dreams. They're fully supported by their partners.'

She'd done her homework, knew the answers without having to think.

'And is that what your friend Makepeace did? Support you?'

'Friend' was loaded, too.

Okay. Hands up. She was the one who'd gone out of her way to give Josh the impression, over the years, that she had a continuous string of boyfriends. Not that he'd taken much interest on his flying visits.

It was as if, after their one night together, he'd totally wiped her from his mind. As if the minute their relationship had changed from friendship to intimacy she'd become just like any other girl he'd ever dated.

Just like the girls she'd once almost pitied because she'd always known he was going to leave the minute he had his degree in his pocket.

Dispensable.

Which made it doubly surprising that he'd remembered Toby's name. They'd only met once as far as she was aware.

'Well,' she said, 'on the plus side, he didn't arrive in the middle of the night like some avenging angel, demanding that I stop being such a fool. Does that answer your question?' Then, tired of playing games, 'I have no idea how Toby felt about Posie, Josh. I didn't discuss what I was doing with him. It was none of his business.'

'That's pretty much what you said to me a year ago.'

'I didn't know…'

Her mouth dried and, suddenly afraid, she held Posie a little more tightly because it had everything to do with him. Maybe, then, if she hadn't responded with outraged anger, but had taken the time to sit down, listen, he might, despite his sworn promise to Michael, have told her the truth.

'You should have told me.'

'What would that have achieved? You were already pregnant.' Then, 'You're quite sure that Posie is mine?'

'What?' That was so far from what she'd been thinking that Grace took an involuntary step back, stumbling against one of the chairs at the work table.

As Posie let out a startled cry, Josh reached out for her and steadied her, then laid his palm against Posie's head, calming her, giving Grace a chance to catch her breath.

'Is she?' he repeated, so intently that she knew without doubt that he wanted it to be so. That, despite his opposition, despite everything, he desperately wanted this little girl to be his child. For a moment it felt as if the world had truly been made over. But the joy swiftly faded into something closer to fear.

Her mother had warned her. *"He seems attached."*

For ten years she'd been living in a fantasy world in which Josh Kingsley was her hero, the boy she'd fallen in love with. But what did she know about the man he'd become? At home he was just Josh, but in the real world he was a power to be reckoned with. A man who'd built an empire from nothing. Who'd broken her heart when he'd brought home a laughing bride, then on his next visit announced, without apparent emotion, that the marriage had been a mistake. A man who other men treated with respect and, maybe, fear. A man who saw only the prize…

She'd wanted him to bond with Posie and, against all the odds, it seemed that he had. Now, too late, she realised that it was not his mother, or hers, who she'd have to fight to keep her baby. It was him.

'I've only your word for that, Josh,' she said, crossing to the buggy and tucking Posie in, fastening her safely, freeing herself for the fight before turning to face him. 'It never occurred to me to doubt you, but maybe we'd both be easier in our minds if we had a DNA test.'

'What? No…'

Not the answer he'd expected, she noted with a glimmer of satisfaction as he took a step towards her.

Her feet wanted to take another step back, keep a safe distance between them, but her head demanded she hold her ground. One step could be put down to shock. Two looked like retreat and this was a moment for standing her ground.

'Just in case Michael came to his senses,' she continued, as if he hadn't spoken. 'That would let you off the hook, wouldn't it?'

She knew that wasn't what he'd meant, but the alternative was too shocking to deserve acknowledgement.

'You made it very clear that you were simply going through the motions to keep him happy,' she said. 'That an actual baby was the last thing you'd anticipated or wanted, and I can understand why you wanted to put a stop to it…'

She faltered, stopped, hearing what she was saying and realising that it wasn't true. She didn't understand. Worse, she was still pretending, still hiding, protecting herself from hurt. But this was more important than her feelings. More important than his.

Overwhelmed by a heart-pounding rush of anger at his selfishness, she said, 'Actually, no, I can't imagine why you'd be that cruel, but then I do have a heart.'

The raw slash of colour that darkened Josh's cheekbones was a warning that she'd gone too far, but she discovered that she didn't give a damn. He'd just insulted her beyond reason and she wasn't going to stand there and take it.

'Unless,' she continued with a reckless disregard for the consequences, 'you really think that I'd cheat my sister, foist a child conceived out of careless passion rather than a clinical donation on a couple so desperate that they would have done anything, even lied to the person they loved most in the world—'

If she'd hit him the effect couldn't have been more dramatic.

'No!' he said, and it was too late to step back as he surged forward, seized her, his fingers biting into her arms. 'No!'

'No what?' she demanded, meeting his fury head-on and refusing to be intimidated, refusing to back down. She owed it to Posie, owed it to herself, to stand up to him.

'No what?' she repeated, when he just stood there, staring at her as if he'd never seen her before. Well, he hadn't. Not like this. Empowered by motherhood and ready to take on the world.

He took a shuddering breath that seemed to come from deep within his soul and then, never taking his eyes off her, said, 'No. I don't need a DNA test. No. I don't want to be let off the hook. No. I don't believe you'd lie to me…' He broke away, as if he couldn't bear to look at her. 'I'm sorry, but when I saw you with Makepeace, his arm around you, you looked like a family and it just all seemed to make perfect sense…'

He looked so utterly wretched and where a moment before she'd been angry, now she didn't know what to think. She only knew what she felt. Grief. Confusion. Fear at the enormous responsibility for a precious life.

And maybe part of her anger was because she suspected he'd been right when he'd accused her of being too scared to risk a relationship, move on, make a life away from the safety of Phoebe and Michael's home.

Had pining after him been the safe option?

'Josh?'

The muscles in his jaw were working as he clamped down to hold back the tears and in a heartbeat the tables were turned. She could weep, but he was a man. Faced with loss, all he could do was get angry, lash out.

He was grieving, too, and just as he'd reached out to her that moment when she'd woken in the kitchen, now she reached out to him.

'I know,' she said, lifting her hand to his face, feeling the silkiness of the close-cut beard against her palm, the bone that moulded the face she knew as well as her own. Every mark, every tiny dint that life had put into it. The creases that bracketed his mouth when he smiled. The white fan of lines around his eyes where the sun never quite reached. The thin scar on his forehead where he'd fallen as a child. 'It's okay to cry.'

And, laying her cheek against his heart, she wrapped her arms around his chest and held him close.

'You're frightened and that's okay. I understand. I'm frightened, too.'

Josh, crushing her to him, didn't think there was a snowball's chance in hell that she understood one damn thing about what he was feeling. She had never understood and why would she when he'd never told her?

She would never know how he'd felt when he'd come home after that first year, expecting to find her waiting for him, green eyes sparkling, the way she'd always been there. Knowing that he'd let her down.

He'd spent the first week away expecting a call from Michael, hauling him back to face up to what he'd done. When that hadn't happened he'd known that Grace had protected him and that had made him feel even worse.

He'd tried to write, but had been unable to write the words he knew she'd want. But he couldn't stay away for ever and he'd known that she'd be waiting for him, eyes shining with that look he hadn't been able to get out of his head. The look in her eyes when he'd kissed her, undressed her, taken her. It was a 'forever' look. A look that would hook a man, haul him in, nail him down, because a decent man couldn't walk away from a look like that. Not from a girl like Grace.

But she hadn't been home when he had pitched up after twenty-four hours travelling with a ring weighing down his pocket. And when she had eventually turned up, only just in time for dinner, she was not alone, but had brought a boyfriend home with her and those sparkling green eyes had been only for him.

And that had been worse. He'd wanted to grab the guy, beat him to a pulp, then drag Grace down to the basement and make love to her until that look was back in her eyes, but only for him.

And better. Because that selfish gene had been consumed with relief.

Relief, as she'd listened to what he'd been doing with less than half an ear, had won. He could relax, knowing that what had happened between them had meant nothing more than a rite of passage for a girl eager to become a woman.

That she hadn't been sitting around waiting for him to come back and claim her, but had moved on from the jewellery stall and, with Michael's help, had rented a small space at the craft centre, had started her own small jewellery-making business. Had her own tiny van to take her to craft fairs.

Had found someone new, someone closer to home, to share her days and nights with.

That night he'd tossed the ring into the rubbish bin in the tiny basement bathroom, cut short his visit, flown back to his new life. Had found his own substitute for Grace. Lovely blonde, blue-eyed Jessie, who'd had him standing in front of a registrar in the blink of her silky lashes. Jessie, who'd realised her mistake and left him just as quickly. Jessie, now happily married to someone who appreciated her, whose face he could barely remember, while Grace...

She didn't understand but, wrapped like this in her arms, drowning in the warm scent of her, a wisp of hair tickling his chin, he wasn't about to argue with her.

'You're tired. Grieving. In shock,' she said.

No. She hadn't a clue...

'And,' she said, lifting her head to look up at him, her clear green eyes demanding nothing less than the truth, 'I suspect you've got bad news for me.'

'Not bad.' He hadn't thought so, but maybe she'd see it differently. He continued to hold her, meeting her unwavering gaze.

'But not good.'

'Mixed,' he said. 'It was pretty much as I thought. Michael instructed his lawyer to draw up new wills for them both. There were some bequests, but the bulk was left to Posie.'

'That's what I expected,' she said impatiently. 'Tell me the rest.'

'His lawyer had advised naming a guardian for Posie and Michael named me without consulting Phoebe.'

'Because you were her biological father.'

'He didn't tell me about the guardianship, Grace, I swear it. I imagine he thought I'd never know, but it must have seemed to him to be the right thing to do. And maybe he hoped that Phoebe would accept that, as his executor, it made sense.'

'But she didn't.'

'How could she?' He wanted her to know that he understood. 'She apparently blew up in the office, reminding Michael, with every justification, that I had been anything but supportive. That you had given birth to Posie.'

'And?' Then, when he couldn't bring himself to say the words, 'Tell me, Josh!'

'Joint custody was suggested as a compromise, but she just said that with us living on opposite sides of the world that was ridiculous. She didn't stay to argue, but left, leaving Michael to wrap up the meeting.'

'So nothing's been settled? It's all still in the air? Open season on Posie?'

'No…' Then, again, 'No. Michael—because you know how loose ends drove him crazy, how he liked everything to be just so—signed his own will, just a temporary measure until they'd talked it through, before he followed her.'

It took a moment for exactly what that meant to sink in and then she said, 'Oh, dear God.' He caught her as her legs crumpled beneath her, held her, but, before he could reassure her, she said, 'She told him, didn't she? That's why they left the hotel so early.' She looked up at him, her face stricken. 'Why Michael went off the road.'

'No—'

'Yes! He was always so careful, but the police said that he

was driving close to the limit on a winding country road. That he couldn't have seen the mud slick that had run off the fields onto the road until it was too late.'

'You can't know that, Grace!'

'They set out before breakfast and I thought it was just because they were so eager to get home. At least I had the comfort of believing they were happy, excited at coming back to their baby, but if she'd told him…'

'Please, Grace, don't do this to yourself.'

'If he'd told her, Josh.' She shook her head as if to drive the desperate thoughts from her mind. 'What state would they both have been in?'

'Maybe they were relieved. Happy that they didn't have any more secrets. Maybe they just wanted to get home so that they could tell you that.' He thought about the calls he'd ignored on his BlackBerry. Had Michael called him, thinking that if everyone knew the truth, he'd be okay with it? 'Listen to me, Grace,' he said, grasping her by the shoulders, shaking her. 'Look at me.'

She obeyed, raising lashes clumped with the tears she'd shed, eyes stricken with grief that tore at his heart.

'Whatever happened is not your fault. You gave them what they wanted most in the world. We both did what we thought was best.'

'Damned with good intentions.'

She rubbed her hand across her cheek, glancing at it in surprise when it came away dry, then straightened, took a step back and, breaking free, said, 'Well, at least you'll have your daughter to console you.'

'Posie is our daughter, Grace. Yours and mine.'

'You keep saying that, but you'll be the one to make all the decisions about her future. To say where she lives. Who looks after her.'

'Phoebe wanted you to take care of her. I want that, too.'

He saw a flash of hope brighten her eyes. 'Then give me

custody, Josh,' she begged. 'As her guardian you can do that, can't you?'

'Yes,' he said, 'but—'

'You could come and see her whenever you want,' she said. 'She could even come and visit you when she's—'

'I could,' he said, cutting her off before she betrayed exactly how little she thought of his ability to make an emotional commitment. 'But I won't.'

He turned to look at Posie, who was watching the spangle of lights spinning across the ceiling, making excited little sounds as she reached up to catch the colours.

He'd been thinking about her ever since the lawyer had told him that Michael had left her in his care.

He'd been so sure that he was going to be able to hand her over to Grace. Put in flying visits, offer advice, be there for them both when they needed him. But basically keeping his distance.

But Michael had wanted him involved, had wanted his little girl to know her father. And as he'd walked back to Grace's workshop it was Posie's smile as she'd grabbed for his beard, her warm baby smell, the joyful way that she stretched for each new sight, experience that had filled his head and he'd known that.

'I'm the only father that Posie is ever going to have and she deserves more than that from me.' He turned to look at Grace, white-faced at the bluntness of his refusal, her hand to her mouth. 'From us.'

CHAPTER EIGHT

GRACE watched him cross to the buggy and crouch beside Posie, catch her tiny hand, hooking it in one of his long fingers—strong, darkly tanned against her pale pink, almost transparent skin. The baby noises grew more excited as she grasped it tightly, kicking her little feet as she smiled up at him.

'This is something we have to do together,' he said. Then, looking back at her when she didn't respond, 'You know I'm right.'

'Do I?'

'Of course you do. You want what I want.'

Grace stared at him.

'Are you sure about that? You never wanted her, Josh. You never wanted children at all. Remember?'

She did. Remembered, as if it were yesterday, the day he'd heard that his father's new wife had given him a baby daughter and he'd said, '...another kid for him to let down...' That no way, never was he going there....

Easy to dismiss as the angry response of a hurting youth, but he'd never changed.

For a moment their eyes met and she saw he was remembering that moment, too.

'It's easy to say you don't want them, Grace, but Posie isn't some faceless baby. She's real.' Then, with a catch in his throat, 'She's mine....'

Grace swallowed, unable to bear the raw love with which he was looking at Posie.

'I'm so sorry, Josh. You never bargained for this.'

'No? The minute I spilled my seed into a plastic cup it was always a possibility. What I hadn't bargained on was the emotional backlash. I told myself that it was anger that kept me away. I'd signed up for Michael's deal with my eyes open, but he'd changed the rules and I'd been used. That you'd been used, too…' He bent and kissed the tiny fingers. 'I clung to that through nine long months, clung to it when she was born, when I ignored Michael's plea to come and stand as her godfather.'

'You convinced us,' she said, a touch shakily.

'Fooled you. Fooled myself. The truth, Grace, is that I knew that if I saw her, I'd never be able to leave her. Let her go. I'd have fought Michael, Phoebe, even you, to keep her.'

'Are you going to fight me now?'

He took one long look at the baby and then rose to his feet. 'I hope not. I want us to be partners in this, not adversaries.'

'How can we? Phoebe was right. You're in Australia, I'm here. Unless you really do expect me to give up everything I have here, come to Australia and be Posie's nanny.'

'You're her mother, Grace. I wouldn't insult you with anything so crude.'

'I'm sorry.' Then, when he didn't elaborate, 'So? What did you have in mind?'

'I told you. A partnership. As Michael and Phoebe's executor it's my responsibility to interpret their wishes.'

'But…'

'We know what they wanted individually. But if they'd both been in full possession of the facts I know that Michael would have wanted you, that Phoebe would have wanted me to be fully involved in her life.'

Grace frowned, trying to make sense of what he was saying, then, giving up, she said, 'The obvious solution is that I keep Posie. You visit any time you like. Move your headquarters to Maybridge if you want to be a full-time father. The world's a global village these days, so everyone says.' Then, when he didn't answer, 'How much simpler can it get?'

'You think that would be simple?'

She shook her head. 'Of course not, but we've established that we both want the same thing. The rest is just details.'

'Not quite. For a start you're assuming that you'll be able to stay in Michael and Phoebe's house.'

'It's Posie's house,' she reminded him. 'Isn't that what you said?'

'The house is part of Michael's estate. It will have to be valued for probate purposes. I'm not up to date with the property market in this area but I do know that prices have rocketed since Michael bought it fifteen years ago. It's certainly going to be in the seven figure bracket.'

'Over two million. One very like it, a couple of doors down, sold last month.'

'Well, that makes it inevitable. Apart from the fact that it's a very large house for just the two of you, with big running costs that would have to come out of the estate, the likelihood is that it will have to be sold to cover inheritance tax.'

'But it's her home,' Grace repeated, bewildered by this sudden turn of events.

'No, it's your home,' he said, but not unkindly. 'Posie's not four months old, Grace. I don't imagine she's likely to notice where she's living for quite some time, do you? Only who she's living with.'

She swallowed down her protest, knowing that he was right. 'What else?' she asked, knowing that there had to be more.

'I'll set up a Trust with the residue to provide adequate funds to care for Posie, pay for her education, provide all her needs, just as Michael and Phoebe would have done.'

'That's just money. Things. Tell me about the important stuff. About who'll hold her when she cries, who'll take her to ballet lessons, hold her hand on her first day at school. I'll be there, but where will you be?'

'Grace…'

'No! I've heard you say a dozen times that you practically live out of a suitcase. Even if you move your office to Maybridge, you'll never be here.'

'You think I can't change?'

'I think you might mean to,' she said. 'I'm sure you'd try. But how long do you really think changing nappies will be enough? How long before the horizon calls? Can Posie's first step compete with that? Her first word? And what happens when she's sick and you're off somewhere communing with a mountain? You're talking about a partnership, but what's the split? Not fifty-fifty, that's for sure.'

'Is that what you're offering?'

'That's my point, Josh. I can't offer anything. I don't have any rights, remember? You hold all the cards.'

'I could change that.'

'Oh…' The fact that he'd actually been thinking that far ahead took the wind right out of her sails. 'How?'

'Very simply. We'll get married, officially adopt Posie so that we have equal rights as her parents. Fifty-fifty,' he said with a wry smile. 'That is what you wanted?'

Grace felt her heart stop.

Marriage? He was proposing till-death-us-do-part, in-sickness-and-in-health, for-ever-and-ever *marriage*?

Everything that she wanted in one package. Josh, Posie… Except, of course, it wasn't and slowly her heart began to beat again.

'That's a huge commitment just to give me what I want, Josh. As her guardian you could simply put her in my care.'

'I could, but that way neither of us would have any real security.'

She frowned. 'What do you think I'd do, Josh? Run away with her?'

'No, of course not.'

'Then what?' she demanded.

'You might meet someone.'

'Someone?' Then, 'If this is about Toby—'

'No. You told me it's over and I believe you, but it's hardly beyond the bounds of possibility that you'll meet some decent man who'll become part of your life and when that happens, it's inevitable that he'll become the father figure in my daughter's life.'

Then stay with me....

The cry from her heart went unheard, unanswered, as he continued, 'I accept everything you say, Grace. Even if I wanted to, I can't shed my responsibilities just like that. Any change is going to take time and, besides, Posie has had enough disruption in her short life. She needs you.'

Far from delight at getting exactly what she wanted, all she felt was a dull ache at this confirmation that when he said marriage, he did indeed simply mean a partnership, but what choice did she have?

'It's going to take a few weeks to sort things out here, too, Josh. Wind up my business.' Then, trying to make a joke of it, 'Maybe you'd better marry me before you go, just in case I get swept off my feet before we join you in Sydney.'

'Join me?' He looked stunned. 'Would you do even that for Posie?' he said, taking her chin in his hand, lifting her face so that she could not avoid amber and grey eyes that were unexpectedly tender.

Not for Posie. For him....

'Australia is just another island, Josh. It's just bigger than the Isle of Man and you have to cross more sea to reach it....'

A shiver ran through her at the thought, but if that was the only way that Posie could be with her father, the only way Josh could be near his daughter, then, for the two people she loved most in the world, she would do it without another thought.

'No.' Josh's response was abrupt and his hand dropped to

his side. 'I'm not asking you to uproot yourself. Leave everything you know.'

'Only marry you.'

That wiped the tenderness from his eyes.

'Only that,' he said. 'In return for your freedom, I'll buy Michael's house from his estate so that you and Posie can stay there.'

He'd buy the house? Just like that? Without having to even think about it?

'And you? Where will you be, Josh?'

When his baby was crying in the night.

When she was alone...

'At work, like any other father,' he replied. 'As you were quick to remind me, I've got commitments that I can't walk away from, but I'll spend as much time in Maybridge as I can, so keep the bed in the basement flat aired.'

Which answered any questions she had about what kind of marriage he had in mind. Could she live with that? Could he? Living on the other side of the world, did he intend to?

'What happens if I tell you to take your partnership and stick it on the wall?'

'She's my child, too, Grace,' he said, not taking the offence she'd intended. 'I'm prepared to do what's necessary so that you can keep her, but I will be part of her life.'

'In other words, if I don't agree I'll have to fight you for custody.'

'You can try.' He tilted one dark brow. 'Do you think you can afford it?'

'Don't you dare threaten me, Josh Kingsley! Phoebe wanted me to take care of Posie. You know that. Michael's lawyer knows it, too.'

'He knows they were going to talk about it. There's nothing in writing,' he pointed out. 'And the last thing Michael did was sign his will, which suggests that, whatever his wife thought on the subject, he was absolutely clear in his own mind.'

'But he didn't know the truth!'

'Whose fault is that?'

She looked away. Not his. And he was right, she didn't have a case. She'd embarked on a surrogate pregnancy with the sworn intention of giving her baby to her sister. Clear evidence that she had no attachment. And Josh could, if she chose to make a fight of it, make it look as if she was clinging to the baby not just as a free meal ticket, but for the roof over her head.

He wasn't threatening her. He didn't need to. He was simply telling it like it was. And what, after all, was he asking of her? Nothing that she'd hadn't, in her deepest heart, wished for with every fibre of her being. To be his wife.

There was a saying.

Be careful what you wish for.

She managed a careless shrug. 'Well, I suppose a paper marriage is just about one step up from being offered a job as her nanny.'

'You don't have the qualifications to be a nanny, Grace. Marry me and you'll keep your baby, keep your home.'

This was surreal, Grace thought. If they were total strangers, it couldn't be any colder.

Grace had scarcely expected him to go down on one knee, declare undying love, but as a proposal of marriage this lacked just about everything.

'That's it?'

'Would you like me to dress it up with fancy words?'

She shook her head. 'No. It's just a business transaction so we'd better keep it plain and honest.' And, since they were being blunt, she said, 'I imagine you'll want the protection of a pre-nuptial agreement?'

'Imagine again. This isn't a short-term contract. We might be on opposite sides of the world, but we'll be together, partners in Posie's life until she's grown up. Independent. After that… Well, I'd consider half my worldly goods well spent in return for my daughter.'

'I don't want your money. Now or ever,' she managed through a throat apparently stuffed with rocks. 'The only currency worth a damn in this exchange is time and love. Can you spare half of that?'

'Posie will have all I have to give,' he assured her. 'What are you prepared to sacrifice?'

Hope. All her dreams... 'Whatever it takes.'

'Then I have your answer.'

'Yes, I suppose you have,' she said.

And that was it. Two people pledging their life to each other, not with a kiss, not to the soundtrack of champagne corks and cheers but with an awkward silence that neither of them knew how to fill.

'Maybe,' she said with forced brightness when her ears were ringing with the silence, empty and hollow as the years that stretched ahead of them, 'since we're in this for the duration, in a year or two, we could pay another visit to the clinic and make Posie a brother or sister.'

He captured her head, leaning into her and, with his lips inches from her own, his eyes molten lead, his voice crushed gravel, he said, 'Sorry, Grace. If you want me to give you another baby, you're going to have to look me in the eyes while I deliver my fifty per cent.'

Someone tried the door. Then knocked.

She didn't move. Couldn't move as he continued to look down at her, his eyes dark, unreadable, drawing her to him like a magnet until they were standing as close as two people could who weren't actually touching. Until she could feel the heat coming from him, warming her through the thin silk of her shirt, through the navy linen trousers. Until her breasts yearned for his touch and her mouth was so hot that in desperation she touched her lower lip with her tongue.

Closer...

'Grace? It's me…' Abby called, tapping again.

It was Josh who spun away from her, crossed to the door and unlocked it.

'Grace,' Abby said, reaching out for her. 'I'm so sorry….'

They hugged wordlessly for a moment, then Grace turned to introduce Josh.

'Abby, I'd like you to meet Josh Kingsley, Michael's brother,' she said. 'Josh, Abby is a genius with enamel.'

'Hello, Abby. Thanks for stepping in to help Grace.'

'No problem. I'm glad to do it. I'm really sorry to hear about your brother.' Then, glancing at her, Abby said, 'You never said he had a beard.'

'It's a temporary aberration,' she said rapidly, before he could wonder just what she had said about him—she couldn't remember saying *that* much, but when you were working together… 'Josh, this is going to be boring. Why don't you take Posie home?'

Josh didn't want to go anywhere. He wanted to stay right here and stare at the gleam of her lower lip where her tongue had touched it. Wanted to rub his thumb over it, lick it, taste her just as he did in his dreams….

'Your mother will probably have arrived by now.'

Not much of an incentive, even if she had trusted him with Posie.

'I'll wait,' he said. Then, before she could object, 'You wouldn't want to disappoint the ducks, would you?'

She looked up and for a moment their eyes closed the distance between them.

Then, without another word, she turned to Abby.

He wandered around her workshop. It was his first visit and he was impressed by the drama, the simplicity of the design, the uniqueness of the display shelves. There was nothing to detract from the jewellery—each piece was individually lit within its own compartment—which alone provided the colour, the richness. Drew the eye.

He touched a collar of gemstones, closing his eyes as he imagined Grace wearing it. Imagined fastening it around her neck… He glanced across at her, head to head with Abby as they went through something on her computer.

As if feeling his eyes on her, she looked up, a slight frown puckering the smooth space between lovely arched brows. Then, as Abby asked her something, she turned back to the computer.

'You never said he had a beard.'

She'd talked about him to her friends?

He rubbed his hand over his chin. A temporary aberration, was it? Maybe…

Posie whimpered. 'What's up, angel?' he said, bending over the buggy. He was rewarded with a smile and an excited wiggle. Did she know him? So soon?

Oh, no. The wiggle had an entirely different cause.

'Grace, Posie needs changing.'

'You'll find everything you need in her bag,' she said, not turning round, but concentrating on the screen. 'Wipes, clean nappy, plastic bag to seal up the used nappy.'

'But—'

'The washroom is behind my office.' Then she did turn round, one exquisitely arched brow challenging him to put all those big sentiments he'd been throwing around, all his pro-testations about wanting to be a father, to practical use. 'Put a couple of towels on my desk.'

He had two choices. Throw himself on her mercy or get on with it. He kicked the brake off the buggy and wheeled Posie into Grace's office, closing the door firmly behind him. He did not need an audience for this.

Then he looked down at Posie.

'It's my first time, kid,' he said. 'Be gentle with me….'

Grace had been holding her breath. As Josh shut the door of her office, she let it go and Abby said, 'Bless.' Then, 'Has he ever changed a nappy before?'

'I shouldn't think so.'

She raised her eyebrows. 'You're that mad about the beard?'

Josh, feeling much as he'd done when he'd secured his first contract—exhausted but triumphant—put Posie to his shoulder and continued his exploration of Grace's workshop. Flipped through sketches for a new design.

Then he saw a fairy-tale confection sitting on a stand.

'Ready?' Grace asked, reaching for Posie, apparently finished with her briefing.

'This is pretty,' he said, picking it up, turning it so that it caught the light. She didn't answer and he turned to look at her. 'Do you get much call for tiaras?'

'Only from brides.'

It was much too late to wish he'd looked the other way, kept his mouth shut. Impossible to just put it down and walk away. 'What stones did you use?' he asked, sticking with practicality.

'Pearls, obviously. Pink jade and quartz to match the embroidery on the bride's dress. Swarovski crystals.'

'Lucky bride,' he said, replacing it carefully on the bench. 'You've come a long way since your first bead necklace.'

'There's more than one way to travel, Josh,' she said, tucking Posie into the buggy. 'Give me a call if you need anything, Abby. Help yourself to the drawing board if you want to work on your own designs.'

'How good is she?' Josh asked as they headed for the park, eager to get the *'bride'* word out of his head.

'She's got real flair. I was going to offer her an exhibition later in the year—nearer Christmas when everyone is looking for something special….'

'Was?'

'I'm not in any position to make promises at the moment. I've got to put Posie first. I need to be able to see a way ahead.'

'You seem to work well together. You obviously trust her.

Is she serious about making a career in jewellery design, or is it a pin-money hobby?'

'She came along to a class after her marriage broke up. Therapy, she said. She obviously doesn't need to work, probably doesn't need the pin money, but you do reach a point at which making jewellery to give away is no longer enough. I think she's passed that.'

'She sounds as if she'd make you an ideal partner.'

Grace stopped, staring at him. 'Partner?'

'You'd halve the workload and costs, double the stock,' he pointed out. 'It's worth thinking about.'

'I can see why you're a tycoon, skimming the stratosphere, while I'm still bumping along on the cobbles.'

'Hardly that. You've obviously managed to maximise all your skills and you have a wonderful selling space,' he said, taking her arm as they crossed the road and entered the park. Then, as he was assailed by the scent of frying onions, he realised just how long it had been since breakfast, 'Mustard or ketchup?'

'What?' Spotting the hot-dog van, she said, 'Oh, no…'

He tutted. 'It's lunch time and you're the one who can't afford to miss meals.'

'It's half past eleven.' Then, with a grin like a naughty schoolgirl, she said, 'Ketchup. No onions. And chips if they've got them.'

'I'll catch you up,' he said, surrendering the buggy.

It was the half-term holiday and the nearest benches were all occupied by mothers watching small children and she wandered alongside the path, following the lake until she was out of sight of Josh. It didn't matter. He'd find her, she thought, trying to remember the last time they'd eaten hot dogs from the park van.

He must have been at university, home for the holidays… Her musings were brought to an abrupt halt by the sight of a small boy teetering dangerously on the edge of the lake as he strained to reach a football that was getting further away from him with every lunge.

Letting go of the buggy, she grabbed the back of his sweater just as gravity won.

'What on earth do you think you're doing?' she said as she hauled him back from, at best, a very cold bath, at worst…

'I can't go home without the ball or my dad'll kill me.'

'Now, is that really likely?' she asked, trying not to think how very much she wanted to shake him herself.

'If he doesn't kill me, my brother will. It's his ball.' Then, looking up at her with big brown eyes, 'You're bigger than me. You could probably reach it.'

They both studied the ball as, driven by a light breeze, it drifted slowly, but inexorably, towards the centre of the lake.

'No one could reach it.'

'You could break a branch off one of those bushes, miss,' the boy suggested helpfully. She wasn't, for a minute, taken in by the 'miss', but even if she had been prepared to indulge in such vandalism, it wouldn't have helped. The ball was too far out for anything but direct action.

She looked around. There was no sign of Josh, but with the children off school there was probably a queue.

She looked again at the ball. While she didn't, for a moment, believe that either his brother or his father would kill him, she did know that, as soon as she turned her back, he'd try to get it himself and, without pausing to consider the wisdom of such a move, she parked Posie by the bench, kicked off her shoes, rolled up her trousers as far as they'd go. Then, with a stern, 'Watch the baby!' she waded in.

A gang of loutish ducks who'd gathered in anticipation of a free lunch flapped away in a flurry of outrage at the invasion, driving the ball even further into the centre of the lake.

'No crusts for you,' she muttered, sucking in her breath sharply at the coldness of the water and doing her best not to think about the slimy stuff oozing over her feet as she took a step towards the centre of the lake. Or how slippery it was. How easy it would be to lose her footing. Instead, she grabbed a low overhanging branch for safety and she eased herself closer to the ball.

Josh, cardboard tray holding cartons of tea, hot dogs, Grace's chips came to an abrupt halt as he saw Posie, parked on the path with a small boy clutching the handle of the buggy. Saw her shoes. Then, as he saw Grace wading out into the lake, his heart turned over.

'What on earth are you doing, Grace?' he thundered.

Josh. *Now* he turned up, Grace thought, wishing she had kept her shoes on as she felt something hard beneath her toes and belatedly thought of all the things that got thrown into the lake.

'Going for a paddle,' she tossed back, without turning round to see if his face matched his voice, afraid that if she made any sudden moves, she'd slip. 'Why don't you roll up your trousers and come on in? The water's lovely.'

'Say that again without your teeth chattering and I might just believe you.'

'Wimp,' she countered, keeping her eye on the ball, which her own movement was driving further towards the centre of the lake.

She didn't need Josh Kingsley to tell her—from the dry vantage point of the footpath—that this was probably the worst move she'd made in a very long time. Too late now, she thought, gritting her teeth as the water edged above her knees and soaked into her trousers.

Then she ran out of branch.

It was much too late to wish she'd stuck to looking helpless on dry land. Instead, she made a sideways tack, taking the long way round to come at the ball from behind.

It was only as she turned to face the path that she realised just how far out she was.

She had no one to blame but herself, she reminded herself

as she scooped up the ball, tucked it under her arm and waded back, grabbing for the safety of the branch.

There was a crack like a pistol shot as it broke off and, before she could save herself, she was sitting up to her armpits in water.

The shock of it drove the breath from her body and, unable to move, unable to speak, unable to think, she just sat there clutching the ball to her chest.

CHAPTER NINE

JOSH abandoned the tray and plunged into the water, grabbed Grace by the arms and hauled her upright. He wasn't sure which of them was shaking the most as he said, 'I'm sorry I was so long. I had to wait for the chips.'

'That's good. That means they're fresh,' she said. 'Hot.' Then, 'Did you remember—'

'Salt and vinegar,' he said, and suddenly he was grinning as he said it. Laughing.

He'd remembered. He remembered everything about her.

Her legs buckling beneath her as she'd climbed off his motorbike the first time she'd ridden pillion.

The happy way she'd danced at her first school disco. Phoebe had asked him to keep an eye on her, something he hadn't been exactly happy about—he'd had bigger plans than babysitting a fourteen-year-old—but she'd been having such a good time that it had made him almost envious.

He remembered the way she'd flung her thin arms around him, her tears soaking into his shirt, when he'd bought her a puppy. The way she'd rolled her eyes at his choice of girls, music, clothes. Her quietness. The way she'd listened to him when he'd told her his dreams…

Remembered her face as he'd left her asleep in the tangled sheets.

She was always there. When he thought of home, it was

always Grace who filled his mind. Always Grace who was the '…ever fixed mark…'

'I remembered,' he said, and her lovely mouth tilted up at the corners, a snort of laughter escaped her because it was beyond ridiculous that two sensible adults would be standing up to their thighs in a muddy lake, talking about chips. 'So, are you done with paddling for the day? Only they'll be getting cold.'

'C-cold?' That made her laugh again so that she was in danger of dropping the ball. He took it from her, turned and tossed the ball to the boy. 'There you go. And keep away from the water in future,' he called after him as he grabbed it and ran.

'H-he d-didn't even say th-thank you,' she said, and that seemed to make her laugh even more.

'No doubt he thought he was in trouble,' he said, picking some waterweed from her shoulder, before taking her hands and helping her back up onto the path. He took off his jacket and wrapped it around her shoulders.

'It'll be ruined,' she protested.

'Then it will be a match for the trousers and the shoes. Here, drink this,' he said, handing her a carton of tea. And they sat dripping on the bench, drinking scalding tea, eating hot dogs.

'Aren't you going to eat the chips?' he asked, taking one. 'They're very good.'

She groaned. 'I shouldn't have vinegar,' she said, looking at them with hungry longing. 'Because of the milk.'

'Right.'

Then, as he took another one, 'I don't suppose one would hurt…'

'Better?' he asked a couple of minutes later as she wiped her fingers on a paper napkin.

'Brilliant,' she said, unpeeling herself from the bench and tossing the rubbish in a litter bin, while he fished out the bag from under the buggy and hurled a handful of crusts far into the lake, sending the birds spinning and flapping to reach it. 'Greedy little beggars. They've no manners.'

'That's what I love about them,' Grace said, watching him, hair blown by the breeze, shirt clinging to shoulders broad enough to prop up her entire world. Muddy trousers, wet shoes where he'd come to her rescue. 'They go for what they want. No pretence. No hang-ups.'

Then, because she didn't want to think about what she couldn't have, she told him about the time Phoebe had used up all the bread, not just to keep her amused, but to annoy her mother.

'Are you telling me that perfect Phoebe was once a terrible teenager?' The idea seemed to amuse him.

'Apparently.' And she smiled, too. 'Once she slipped away when we were packing up to move. She took the bus into town and didn't come back until dark, forcing everyone to stay another night.'

'I'll bet that made her popular.'

'Most of the kids loved the freedom, but Phoebe just wanted to have a proper home. After that, Mum called someone she'd known at school, got her a pocket-money job as a home help with bed and board and a part-time business course at the local college. She never looked back.'

'And you? Was that what you wanted?'

'I didn't know what I wanted.' In hindsight, though, she could see why her mother had decided to leave her with Phoebe once she'd been released from custody. She must have known it was only a matter of time. 'Thanks for jogging my memory,' she said, when she realised he was waiting for more. 'Perfection would have been an impossible ideal to live up to.'

'You think?' He took her hands. 'I don't believe you have a thing to worry about on that score, Grace,' he said, his grip tightening, his gaze suddenly more intense. 'You were born a giver. Ducks. Kids with lost balls. A sister desperate for a baby. You're always there.' Then, rubbing his thumbs over the backs of her fingers, 'And, speaking of giving, you'll need a ring. Do you want to design it yourself? Or will you allow me to choose something for you?'

'There's no need for that,' she said. A ring was a symbol, a token of deep and abiding love. Then, because that sounded ungrateful, 'It seems…inappropriate to make a big thing of this.'

'Because it's so soon?'

Josh had known from the moment the facts had been laid out in the lawyer's office what he had to do. Maybe he'd known it from the beginning. He'd told himself that it was no more than a piece of paper that gave Grace back her baby. It wasn't as if he'd planned to repeat the mistake of marrying a woman who'd want more than he could give.

Then, coming around the corner, seeing her wading out into the lake, imagining glass, rusty cans, imagining her slipping and getting tangled up in weeds or rubbish while he was stranded on the path, hands full, unable to move, it had hit him, like running full tilt into the Rock of Gibraltar.

That he didn't want a paper marriage—he wanted Grace. Had always wanted Grace.

Now, hearing the hesitation in her voice, he wanted to wrap his arms around her, kiss away her doubts, put that laughter back into her eyes. Somehow reassure her that if she'd give him the chance, he would strive to make her happy. Give her all the children she wanted, with love, passion, the two of them becoming one in that precious moment of conception.

Instead, he did the very opposite, because to say those things would be selfish beyond belief. In two weeks, three at the most, he'd be on the other side of the world and she'd be on her own, picking up the pieces, making a life for their little girl, while he came and went as he always had, pleasing himself.

The one selfless thing he could do was give her Posie. A home that would be hers for ever. Security.

She deserved that. They owed it to her—Michael, Phoebe and, above all, him.

'People will understand,' he said.

Grace, her hands clasped in his, understood just one thing. Josh didn't have to do this. He was, incredibly, doing it for her. That he was everything she'd ever wanted and now they had a common purpose that would bind them together more tightly than fleeting passion.

'How soon?' she asked.

'I'd like to settle everything before I leave.'

Grace remembered the way he'd made lists on a lined pad—an organisational skill he'd learned from Michael. He'd numbered each item, ticking it off as each task was accomplished so that he could forget it, move on.

And she had, of course, copied her hero.

It was a good system. It kept you focused on what was important. But the idea of being an item on a list, something to be ticked off, was so mortifying that she said, shivering, 'Leave it to me. I'll contact the registrar when we get home and check what we need to do.'

'Let's worry about that later. You need to get home and out of those wet things.

They went in the back way through the mud room. Grace hung up Josh's jacket so that the lining could dry while Josh eased off his wet shoes, peeled off his socks, tossed them in the sink while she struggled with the buttons of her own jacket.

'Here, let me do that,' he said, bending to tackle them, so that she was staring at his thick, dark, wind-tousled hair.

He peeled it away from her shirt, draped it over the draining board, then, while she was still struggling to catch her breath, slipped the button at her waist. The zip, always dodgy, peeled back under the added weight of water and the lot fell in a crumpled heap at her feet.

'I can manage,' she said, kicking free of her trousers, slapping his hand away as he set to work on her shirt, clearly believing her incapable of undressing herself.

'Sure?' he said.

'P-positive…' Even if she had to rip it off. 'If you leave your trousers, I'll put them through the wash….'

Her mouth dried as, taking her at her word, he slipped the buckle on his belt, undid the button at his deliciously narrow waist and slid down the zip.

Later. She'd meant later, she thought as she groped for the door handle, backing into the kitchen. She was almost sure she'd meant later, she told herself as she turned and found herself face to face with her mother, who was at the table preparing vegetables. Josh's mother, who was watching her.

While Grace stood there, too embarrassed to speak, Josh eased her aside so that he could push Posie into the kitchen, then, looking round, said, 'This is probably a good moment to tell you all that Grace and I are getting married as soon as we can make arrangements.'

Josh's mother reacted first.

'Married? Well, congratulations, Grace. And at least no one will put the obvious construct on the unseemly haste since you've already had the baby.' Then, while Grace was still cringing with embarrassment, she turned to Josh. 'I suppose you'll be giving her my grandmother's engagement ring, too?'

About to step in and read his mother the riot act, he saw the compassion in Grace's eyes and realised that she had seen what he, on the defensive, protecting himself and Grace from her barbs, had missed. How, looking beyond the plastic surgery, the perfectly applied make-up, the exquisite black designer suit, his mother was a fragile, desperately unhappy woman who'd just buried her oldest son—a son she'd lost years before.

'Would you look after Posie for me, Mrs Kingsley,' Grace added, 'while I go and take a shower?'

And he saw how like Phoebe she was.

Her gentleness. Goodness.

She would never look back with regret on an unkindness. Cling to hostility, as both he and Michael had done. And he knew at that moment that he wouldn't want to die with that leaden weight in his heart.

He wheeled the buggy closer to his mother, touched her shoulder and said, 'I'll take your bag upstairs, while you and Dawn get to know your granddaughter.'

His reward was a smile from Grace. It was a moment of revelation. Truth.

'Mum?' Grace prompted, obviously wanting to get any unpleasantness out of the way in one fell swoop. 'Have you anything to say?'

'Only… What happened to your clothes?'

'What are you looking for?'

Grace looked up as her mother stood at the study door. 'My birth certificate. I know it's here somewhere because I had to get a copy when I needed a passport for a school trip to France.'

'I didn't know you'd been to France. You've never mentioned it.'

'No…' She'd spent the week before the trip in a state of rising panic. On the surface she'd been just as excited as all the other kids in her class, but deep down she'd known with a cast iron certainty that when she got back everything would have shifted. That it wouldn't be Phoebe, but some stranger from Social Services waiting for her… 'I was sick the morning we were due to leave and couldn't go,' she said.

'That's a pity.'

'It happens…' Then, looking back at the drawer, she saw her name typed on a neat tab and lifted the surprisingly thick folder from its sling, put it on the desk and opened it. 'Good grief.'

'What is it?'

'My entire life, apparently.'

At least everything that related to her life since she'd come into Michael's house. Correspondence with Social Services, the Parental Responsibility Order they'd applied for when she had come to live with them. All those horrible Grace-tries-so-hard-but…end of term school reports.

She'd known a lot of stuff—far more about some things than the other kids—but not in an organised, exam passing way. But she'd shone in art and that had got her a place at the local tech.

And then, at the back, tucked away in plastic wallets, she found her medical card, passport and, finally, her birth certificate.

She took it out, unfolded it on the desk and looked at this public record of who she was. Wondered what a stranger would make of it. Josh, even.

Date and place of birth: 28 July 1980, Duckett's Farm, Little Hinton.

Actually, in a van illegally parked in a field at Duckett's Farm. She'd been told the tale a hundred times. How Grace Duckett, ignoring her husband's fury at having a dozen New Age 'travellers' pull over and set up camp on one of his fields when her mother had gone into labour, had been so generous, so kind that, instead of being called Aurora, a twist on her mother's name, she'd been called Grace after the farmer's wife. As a little girl she'd longed for the exotic Aurora. These days she was deeply grateful to Grace Duckett.

Name: Grace Louise.

She turned to her mother. 'Who was Louise?'

'One of the women in our group. A herbalist. She helped me with your birth.'

'I don't remember her.'

'You wouldn't. She met someone at a music festival and settled down with him in a semi somewhere near Basingstoke.'

'Oh. Right.' She turned back to the document.

Father: Steven Billington, wood-carver.
Mother: Dawn McAllister.

'Did you ever hear from him?' she asked. 'My father? Ever try to find him? For maintenance?'

Her mother shook her head. 'What would have been the point? He'd found someone else, they had a baby and he never did have any money. It hurt, but that's how life is, Grace.' She smiled. 'I loved him enough to let him go.'

As she'd let Phoebe go. And her.

'I can't let Posie go,' she said. 'I've lost so much....'

'I'll stay as long as you need me,' her mother promised. 'Once you're married...'

'It's just a piece of paper,' she said, not even bothering to pretend to her mother.

'For Josh, maybe.' Her mother touched her shoulder. 'You always did light up around him, Grace.'

What could she say? Denying it wouldn't change anything. Or convince her mother.

'It seems indecent to be even thinking of a wedding so soon after burying Michael and Phoebe. Almost like dancing on their graves.'

'The human spirit needs to affirm life at these dark moments, Grace. To celebrate new beginnings. Rebirth.'

'We weren't planning on a celebration. A ten minute in-and-out job at the register office rather than a fertility ceremony,' she replied. Then wished she'd kept her mouth shut. 'Josh has to get back to Australia as quickly as possible. He's just got some big new contract in China.'

'You're not going with him?'

'He'll be all over the place and I've got commitments here. The house. My business...'

'I'll keep the fertility dance on hold for the time being, then.'

'That's probably wise,' Grace replied. 'At least until you've had your hips fixed.'

Her mother laughed out loud at that, then said, 'So? What are you going to wear?'

'Wear? I hadn't thought about it.'

She didn't want to think about it. About the design for a tiny sparkly tiara that she'd drawn years ago and never made. About walking down the aisle in the dream dress on the dream day when she married her dream man.

'It's not important.' And, firmly changing the subject, she said, 'Were you looking for me for something special?'

'Oh, yes.' Her mother opened the book she was holding and handed it to her. 'I've been looking for some way to commemorate Phoebe and Michael. I know a man who carves words into slate stepping stones and I thought maybe a quotation from this one. Elizabeth Barrett Browning…'

Grace recognised it instantly. Had learned it by heart years ago at the height of her teenage infatuation with Josh. She had no need to read it, but closed her eyes and said the words out loud. '"How do I love thee? Let me count the ways…"' But when she came to the final line, it was Josh who completed the poem.

'"—and, if God choose, I shall but love thee better after death."'

Her eyes flew open and he was there, standing right in front of her, and she swayed towards him.

'Steady,' he said, catching her. 'Standing with your eyes closed can do crazy things to the balance.'

'I'm fine,' she said. She wasn't. But she would be.

'Right.' And after a moment he let go of her. Then, taking the book from her hand, he turned to Dawn. 'That last line. It's perfect.'

'I thought so.'

'You do understand, Dawn? Why we're getting married so quickly.'

'You're giving Posie a family,' she said. 'That's a noble thing, which is entirely different from being solemn about it.' She lifted her hand to his cheek. 'You're allowed to be happy, too.'

'Mum…' Grace warned, afraid she was going to start on her

earth mother, circle of life, fertility thing again. 'I called the registrar, Josh. We need some paperwork. Birth certificates…'

'And?'

'Your decree absolute.'

He nodded. 'I've got them both at home. I'll get Anna to courier them overnight.'

Anna, the personal assistant.

She slammed the door on that thought and said, 'Right. Good. So all we have to do is call in at the register office, present the necessary documents and give sixteen clear days notice of our intention to marry.'

'Sixteen days? I thought maybe a week…'

'Is that going to be too long? Once we've given notice, we have a year in which to go through with it. If it's not convenient, we could wait…'

Josh put down the book and took out his new BlackBerry. 'It's going to be tight. Let's see. It's the twenty-seventh tomorrow…' he checked the diary '…which makes the first available day the twelfth of June. I have to be in Beijing on the fifteenth… It's just do-able. I was coming to London next week for meetings. I've managed to bring them forward.'

'Not too much of an inconvenience then,' she said.

'No…' He made a note, then slipped it back into his pocket.

When he looked up he realised that both Grace and her mother were staring at him.

'I think I'll go and see what Laura is doing,' Dawn said, picking up her book and heading for the door.

Josh didn't take his eyes off Grace.

'I've just been incredibly insensitive, haven't I?'

He'd watched a variety of expressions chase across her face since she'd opened her eyes when he'd finished her poem.

She'd hadn't been this easy to read since she was a girl, he realised. All those years ago, he'd watched her putting on a brave face for Phoebe, but it had been obvious to him that she was scared out of her wits at the prospect of facing a new school. He knew she was right to be scared. Knew how bad it could be for anyone arriving in the middle of the school year when friendship groups had been established.

And she had 'outsider' written all over her.

She was a quick study, though. Maybe it was living in the wild, but she'd been swift to adapt, learning the most acceptable labels to have on her clothes, the right way to fix her hair. And that most vital survival technique—how to keep her feelings under wraps.

Right now there was too much going on. Too many feelings to hide. He'd just had a glimpse of one more loss she was being forced to bear, this time by him.

He wished he could blame his complete boorishness on the fact that he'd retreated to the basement to deal with things that could not be put off. He'd had to reorganise meetings, arrange for busy colleagues to stand in for him, reassure his Chinese partner that he was going to be there to hold his hand at the next round of meetings with the bureaucrats, but it wasn't that.

It was the glow that had lit her up as she'd recited that poem listing every way in which a woman could love a man, knowing that he could have had that if he'd cared about anyone but himself.

'You don't have to answer that,' he said. 'I already know the answer.'

Grace sighed. 'It's all right, Josh. You don't have to pretend with me. We both know that you're only doing this so that I can keep Posie. I'm truly grateful.'

Pretend?

Grateful...

'Dammit, Grace, you don't have to be grateful.'

He turned away, raking his hands through his hair, locking his fingers behind his head to keep them from reaching out to touch her lovely face. From telling her what she truly meant to him. Telling wouldn't do it. He was going to have to show her....

'I'm the one who's grateful and I'll say now what I should

have said earlier.' Then, because some things had to be said face to face, he dropped his hands, turned to look at her. 'You're the mother of my child and I'll do my best, whatever it takes, to make you happy.' And in a gesture that he'd have sworn was completely alien to him but now seemed as natural as breathing, he laid his hand on his heart. 'You have my word.'

She looked up at him, her heart in her eyes. 'Anything?'

It was what, when he'd challenged her, forced her to face reality, he'd demanded of her. He could offer no less.

'Anything,' he affirmed with all the conviction he could muster. Then, rather more gently, 'Tell me, Grace.'

'Well, it's just that I was wondering if we could hold the actual wedding ceremony somewhere other than the register office.' This was so far from what he'd been expecting that he was left floundering for something to say. 'It's where I had to go to register Michael and Phoebe's deaths…'

She faltered, clearly unable to find the words to express what that had done to her.

She didn't have to.

She shouldn't have had to ask. He should have thought, at least discussed it with her.

'I'm sorry, Josh. You've got more than enough on your plate without me being a pathetic wimp about something so unimportant—'

'Don't!' He caught her to him, held her close. 'It's important to you and that makes it important to me. I should have talked this through with you instead of just assuming that because it's the simplest solution it's the right one.'

'But it is. Simple is good. Just…'

'Just not that simple.' He leaned back a little so that he could look at her. So that she could see that he meant what he said. 'It's not a problem. We can have the ceremony wherever you like.'

'Thank you.' Her smile was exactly like the one she'd given him when he'd tossed her his spare crash helmet. Thrown her a lifeline… 'I'm sure we could find somewhere with a licence that isn't all white doves and string quartets,' she added and, with her this close, looking up at him as if he were her white knight, he felt a surge of hope that this could, truly, be more than a paper marriage.

More than hope.

An almost unbearable need to kiss her, show her that if only she would take her courage in both hands, trust him…

Trust. It kept coming back to that. He had asked her to trust him and she had, despite the fact that he'd not walked, but had run from her after that night when she'd given him everything.

He'd told himself that it had been the right thing for her, but it been his own fear, the prospect of his vaunting ambitions being hampered by a girl who needed more than he could ever give that had sent him out into the cold dawn.

Rebuilding the trust that he'd shattered so selfishly would have to be earned with bone-deep commitment. Kisses would have to wait.

'What exactly have you got against doves, Grace?'

'Well,' she began, quite seriously, 'for a start they're not ducks…' Then she shook her head and without warning that smile hit him again. 'You know what I mean.'

'Yes, I know,' he managed. 'Simple.'

'I thought that's what you wanted, too. Especially as you'll be flying off to China the minute the ink's dry on the certificate.'

Josh hadn't thought about what might happen after the event. Now he did. Did she expect them to say their vows and go their separate ways? That he'd have his bag packed and the taxi waiting to take him to the airport? The idea so appalled him that he said, 'Perhaps not the *very* minute. I thought I'd wait until the following morning. Just for appearance's sake,' he added when she started nervously. 'We both know that the wedding is no more than a formality but there's no reason to share that fact with the rest of the world. In fact, I think your mother might have a point.'

'She might?' she squeaked. 'And what point would that be?'

'That there's a fine distinction between a quiet wedding and something that is, to all intents and purposes, invisible.'

Invisible meant the marriage would pass unnoticed. He suddenly discovered that he wanted the entire world to take note. Having always steered well clear of the gossip column lifestyle, right now he'd actively welcome the prospect of a ten-page spread in *Celebrity*.

'We will need two witnesses. And convention suggests I should have a best man. Maybe,' he said, 'Posie would like to be your bridesmaid?'

'My bridesmaid? That would be the person who's supposed to lead me astray on my hen night, help me with my make-up, carry my train and catch the bouquet?'

'You could have one of those, too. Posie is going to need a little help.'

'I don't think so.'

'Don't be a spoilsport. She'd love being dressed up in pink frills.'

'Oh, please,' she said, trying not to laugh, but a giveaway dimple appeared in her cheek. How could he have forgotten that dimple?

'You think pink is too much of a cliché?'

'You don't want to know what I think.'

'You do know that she'll hold it against you. When she's older. Feel deprived. Just ask her...' Then, 'Where is she?'

'Asleep,' Grace said firmly, the dimple back under control. 'I put her upstairs after lunch so that she wouldn't be disturbed.' Right on cue, there was a gurgle from the baby monitor sitting on the desk. 'Was asleep,' she said. 'I have to go.'

He caught her hand. 'Leave the wedding arrangements to me, Grace. I'll organise everything.'

'I thought you had to be in London all next week for meetings?'

'All you'll have to think about is what you're going to wear,' he said. 'I promise.'

'No problem. I'll have that navy-blue trouser suit cleaned. It'll be perfect.'

CHAPTER TEN

For a moment Josh actually believed her. Then Grace laughed and said, 'I'm going to give Posie a bath before teatime. You can be in charge of the plastic ducks if you promise not to say another word about her being a bridesmaid.'

'You asking me to help?'

'You've already proved yourself in the nappy department. Bathing is next on the agenda. If you can spare the time?'

'Yes… Thank you.'

'Save your thanks until afterwards.'

'How hard can it be?' he said with a flippancy that earned him another smile. One that suggested he'd just said something very foolish. That was okay. Making a fool of himself would be a small price to pay for raising one of her precious smiles.

Actually, it wasn't that difficult. Between them, Grace and Posie made short work of cutting him down to size.

'You undress her while I run the bath,' Grace said.

Easier said than done. He was still wrestling with a minute vest when Grace came looking for him.

'The water's going cold while you two are playing,' she said, leaning against the door, apparently enjoying the spectacle of him reduced to a wreck by an infant.

'I'm not playing,' he protested. Playing he could do. 'It's Posie.' Then, 'No. It's me.' His hands were too big and Posie was so small, her skin so delicate. 'She's so tiny.'

'Oh, please. She's a great big hulk,' Grace said, picking her up with the confidence of practice. Kissing her, then gently tugging the little vest over her head, pausing for a quick peekaboo, before pulling it free, then kissing her again. 'You should have seen her when she was first born,' she said, then looked away, clearly afraid that she'd said something hurtful.

'I wish I had been, too, Grace.' Been there at the birth to hold her hand, do whatever it was that useless men did while the women they loved suffered to give them sons, daughters. Except that would never have happened. He'd have been the outsider, excluded, while Phoebe and Michael supported her through the birth.

She put a hand on his arm, rubbed it gently in a gesture of comfort. 'The first time Phoebe let me bath Posie I was certain I was going to drop her.'

And in that one brief phrase—'Phoebe let me'—she told him that she knew. Understood.

'It's just a question of holding gently but firmly,' she went on as if she'd said nothing of importance. 'Come on. You'll soon learn.'

The small baby bath was on a low stand and Grace sat on a stool with Posie on her lap. She gently washed her face and only then did she lower the baby into the water. Posie immediately went rigid with excitement, then drew back her little legs and kicked.

Water erupted over the end of the bath, where he was poised with a bright yellow plastic duck, hitting him full in the chest.

Posie screamed with pleasure and, while he was looking down at the damage, she did it again, this time showering his head.

He was kneeling in water, was soaked to the skin and his hair was dripping down his back. It was the second time that day he'd been soaked. The second time that they had been laughing together.

Half an hour later he left a smiling, composed Posie, dressed in a tiny white T-shirt and soft blue overalls, in complete command of the nursery while he retreated, dripping, to the basement. Dripping but wrapped in the warmth of the towel Grace had taken from the heated rail and draped around his neck.

'You'll soon get the hang of it,' she said, and he felt like the victor at some ancient games who'd just been garlanded with laurels. 'Next time you'll be ready for her.'

Personally, he didn't care how wet he got if he could be shoulder to shoulder with Grace as, together, they'd bathed their baby.

The undercurrent of tension that had seemed to stretch to breaking point since he'd been home had completely evaporated in the splashing, the laughter, the play of Posie's bath time.

'Ready for her? You mean, you knew that this was going to happen?' He indicated his sodden T-shirt and trousers.

'Why do you think I chose the end that doesn't kick?'

'Oh, I see.' He bent to tickle Posie, who was sitting like a little princess in the crook of her mother's arm, to kiss her downy head. 'I think your mummy set me up.'

'It's a rite of passage,' Grace said, still laughing, as he straightened. Then, as he looked down at her, the laughter died away and in that instant it was as if the last ten years had never happened. They were both still young, untouched, with all their dreams intact.

He was twenty-one, about to embark on the greatest adventure of his life so far, skirting around unsettling feelings for this girl he'd watched out for ever since she'd arrived in his life. A girl who'd come downstairs to bring him a pair of cufflinks she'd made for him, to say goodbye. Except they hadn't been able to say goodbye. Instead, her huge green eyes had provoked an explosive, straight-to-hell physical response that neither of them had had the will or desire to resist.

Her green eyes had that same look now and the effect was, if anything, more devastating. But older, just a touch wiser, he recognised it for what it was. Need, fear of change, of losing someone you care for—only this time it was not him she was afraid of losing, but Posie. And he stepped back, turned away before he embarrassed them both.

Dawn met him as he crossed the hall. 'I was going to ask you how you got on, but I can see,' she said, laughing. 'You're having a very wet day.'

'I'm not complaining,' he said, pulling the towel from around his neck and rubbing at his hair.

'Seize every moment, Josh. They grow up far too quickly.' Then, 'Your mother was talking about ringing an agency to engage a nanny.'

'A wedding planner would be more use right now.' Then, 'No, forget I said that. Grace wants simple.'

'I thought you had simple,' she said.

'Simple,' he said, 'but more complicated.' Then, hearing Grace at the top of the stairs, 'Let's go into the sitting room,' he said. 'Can I get you a drink?'

'I don't,' she reminded him. 'But you go ahead.'

He poured himself a Scotch, sat on the leather footstool that wouldn't suffer from his damp clothes.

'Grace isn't happy with the idea of having the ceremony at the register office,' he said. 'It has too many negative associations. And, since we've decided to invite a few more people, we're going to need somewhere that can provide lunch.' Actually, that was his idea, but she hadn't out-and-out vetoed it. 'Any thoughts?'

'To be honest, Josh, very few of the people I know actually bother with the paperwork. I didn't myself.'

Her sigh was, he thought, unconscious.

'Do you regret that?'

'Maybe. Not that it would have made any difference. Once a man's eyes begin to wander there isn't enough paper and ink in the world to keep him from following them. I wish he'd made an effort to keep in touch with the girls.'

'It must have been hard for you.'

He found it difficult to imagine this slender woman taking on a bunch of thugs who'd been hell-bent on destroying her home. But that must have been easy compared with giving up her precious girls so that they'd have a more settled life than the one she'd chosen for herself.

'I managed. Mostly.' She smiled. 'It's different for the two of you, of course. You're marrying to give Posie a family.'

'I thought it would make adoption simpler, especially in view of the fact that we live in different hemispheres.'

'Maybe that's the problem you need to address,' she said, giving him a very straight look.

'We both have commitments, Dawn,' he said, staring into the glass he was holding as if that somehow held the answer. 'Maybe later…'

'So what's the rush to get married?' She tilted her head to one side, looking for all the world like a small, brightly plumaged bird. 'What are you afraid of, Josh?'

'Of losing her.' The words slipped out. He hadn't intended to say them, but there it was. Plain and honest.

'Posie? Or Grace?'

'Both of them.' He glanced up. 'You do know that she's Posie's natural mother?'

'Not just the shell, but the egg, too? How generous. I'm so proud of her.'

'You raised an amazing daughter, but one who, right now, has no legal rights as far as Posie is concerned. Michael named me as Posie's guardian in his will.'

'And why would he do that?'

'Because Posie is my biological daughter, too, Dawn. Michael had problems of his own…'

'I see.'

'Do you? I'm doing what I can to give Grace a legal right to her own child.'

'While protecting your own?'

'You think that's selfish?'

'I think it's a very natural instinct,' she said, which didn't answer his question. Or maybe it did. Maybe instinct, the urge to survive was, at heart, selfishness. 'But thank you for telling me. It explains a great deal.' She tilted her head again. 'Although not, perhaps, everything.'

'Everything is, for the moment, beyond me, Dawn. I'm adrift. I can't cry. I feel guilty when I forget for a moment…' He looked up. 'Guilty for not being here. If it wasn't for Grace and Posie…'

'Love is the most powerful emotion there is, Josh.'

Love?

'It gives us the strength to hold on long after reason suggests that all is lost. The courage to let go when it feels as if you're tearing your heart out.'

'I let go once. I convinced myself that it was the right decision but I've come to realise that it was a mistake.'

Was he making a mistake now? Still being ruled by that selfish gene?

'How do you know?' he asked. 'How can you tell?'

'Ask yourself who will gain most from the choice you make. Who will be hurt. Whose happiness you truly care about.'

'It's that easy?' he said with a wry smile.

'I didn't say it was easy. Being honest with yourself is the hardest thing in the world. But if you truly love someone, you'll have the courage to face the truth.' Then, 'But you wanted me to help you find somewhere for the wedding. Why don't you go and get into some dry clothes while I take a look at the local paper? That might give me some ideas.'

'You won't mention any of this to Grace? I told her that all she'd have to do was turn up and say "I do",' he said, getting up, then moving to help her as she struggled to get off the sofa.

'Wretched hip,' she muttered.

'How bad is it?'

'A bit like Melchester Castle. A crumbling ruin.' Then, waving away his concern, 'Did you know that they hold weddings there?'

'In the ruin?'

She gave him a look that he recognised. Grace didn't look much like her mother, but that cool, please concentrate, I'm being serious, look was familiar from a hundred teasing exchanges.

How he'd missed that.

Missed her.

'I know they hold those big glossy affairs in the manor house that was built much later,' he said hurriedly.

'They also have a folly—a mini Greek temple affair—that overlooks the lake. I believe they hold less formal weddings there. I'll make some enquiries.' Then, 'And, to answer your question, no, I won't mention this to Grace. She's just about holding herself together for Posie. Anything that feels like a celebration is beyond her.'

'I can understand that. At least she was here…'

'That was not your fault, Josh. You'll honour Michael and Phoebe's memory far more by bringing up his daughter than by standing in church, singing hymns.' Then, patting his hand, 'It's hard when you're young. Everything is so sharply defined. Right, wrong. Black, white. Pleasure, pain. As you get older you realise that life is mostly a greyish muddle and the best you can do is embrace each moment, learn each lesson and move on.'

'Easier said than done.'

'You can't change anything that's happened. Regret is futile. Only the future matters.'

'I wish there was more time but I don't know when I'll get back and I don't want to leave Grace in limbo. I want her to feel safe.'

'Don't worry. Between us we'll make it as painless as possible. Give her a wedding that at the moment she can't allow herself to believe she has a right to enjoy.'

'Thank you. I'll arrange a credit card for you, Dawn. Do whatever you think best. Invite whoever you think she'd want to be there. Just—'

'Keep it simple.'

'Actually, I was going to ask you to make sure my mother doesn't get carried away.'

'Don't worry, I won't let her sell the exclusive to *Celebrity*.'

He managed a smile.

He'd never given Dawn much thought in the past but now he thought he was going to like her rather a lot. Then, remembering Grace's very specific reservations, 'And absolutely no string quartets or doves.'

Josh had been dreaming. It was the same dream that had haunted him for years. Grace, sensuous, silky, fragrant and forever—tormentingly—out of reach.

He'd come awake with a start and for a moment he just lay there, almost awake, not sure where he was.

Then his memory kicked in and the past week came rushing back like a news bulletin that he couldn't switch off. The loss of his brother, the discovery that Posie was not only his daughter, but Grace's, too.

The first small steps towards reconciliation with his mother. He wouldn't let one more night pass without making his peace with his father.

Now he had to face something bigger. His marriage to Grace. The fact that in two weeks she would make a vow that tied her to him. That she would be coming to him, not as a bride should in a once-in-a-lifetime gown, a delicate tiara sparkling like raindrops in her elfin hair as she walked towards him down the flower-decked aisle of the local church, but in a ten-minute ceremony in some mock Greek temple.

Not with her heart in her hands, but to be tied to him by a paper marriage because there was no other way she could keep her baby.

His in name, but still forever out of reach.

He threw back the sheet, sat on the side of the bed, his face in his hands.

As he'd walked back from the lawyer's office, everything had seemed so simple. He and Grace would get married, they would bring Posie up together. She had, after all, said she'd do anything and he'd hoped, believed that their baby would bring them together.

And then he'd walked into her workshop and she'd been wrapped around the guy she'd brought to dinner the last time he'd been home.

Funny, attentive, too good-looking by half, he'd known then that Toby Makepeace was the man who was going to take Grace from him once and for all.

He'd told himself, as he'd flown away, his heart like lead in his chest, that all he wanted was for her to be happy. Had waited, expecting every phone call, every e-mail from Michael to tell him that they were engaged.

Instead, he'd got a phone call from Michael telling him that Grace was going to act as a surrogate mother for Phoebe. The unspoken subtext a silent reminder that he had sworn to keep his role in that pregnancy a secret.

In his desperation, knowing that she was carrying his child, he'd clung to the one small crumb of comfort in the whole business—that if she'd loved Toby Makepeace, it would have been his baby she would have wanted. Taking reassurance from the fact that when she had Mr Perfect at her feet, Grace had still been looking for something more and there was still hope that one day she'd look up and see him, waiting for her, to let go of the side of the pool, cast off, swim out of her depth to join him…

He'd never truly understood her fear. Only now began to have a glimmer of why, after a childhood spent being dragged around by her hippie mother, Grace had clung to this house as her rock, her refuge.

He, on the other hand, had begun life with certainty only to have it ripped out from under him. He didn't cling, didn't believe in roots put down by other people, but instead had spent every day since his parents deserted him plotting his escape, eager to travel the globe, build his own world. One that no one could ever take from him.

He'd thought he had that. Had everything.

He got up, pulled on tracksuit bottoms, a T-shirt, needing air. But, as he came up from the basement and heard Posie's thin wail float down the stairs, he knew that he'd been fooling himself. That the universe was nothing beside the power of a love you would gladly die for and he took the stairs to the nursery two at a time.

The only light spilled in through the doorway, gleaming off the thin silky wrap that floated above her bare feet, giving a glimpse of ankle as Grace turned to look at him. He quickly looked up but her face was in the shadows, all dark hollows around her eyes, in her cheeks that told of nights without sleep.

'Josh… I'm sorry if we disturbed you.'

'No. I was awake. How long have you been up?'

She shook her head. 'I don't know. Half an hour, maybe longer. I thought she was hungry….'

She was trying to coax the baby with a bottle but Posie, fractious, turned away, refusing to take it and all he could think was that he must do something.

Be a father.

'What can I do?'

Grace shook her head. 'I don't know. I was just about to go and wake my mother.'

'You're that worried?' He moved closer.

'She had two of us. She's got to know more than me.'

'Let me take her for a while.'

She surrendered Posie without an argument and he laid the infant against his shoulder where she clung to him, snuffling and nuzzling into his neck like a tiny puppy, for a moment quiet. Then she pulled away and resumed her miserable little grizzle.

Grace hadn't moved. 'Do you think she might be sick? Maybe we should call the doctor?'

We.

Such a small word to mean so much.

He felt Posie's cheeks. 'She's not hot,' he said. 'I think she's just like the rest of us. Feeling the strain. In need of comfort.'

'Who isn't?' she snapped, then, as he put his arm around her, she collapsed against his other shoulder and for a moment, with both arms full—even if both shoulders were getting wet—his world seemed complete. 'I don't know what to do!'

He rubbed his hand against her back, feeling the warmth of her skin through the thin silk. Silk?

'Where's Phoebe's robe?' he asked. Grace was a couple of sizes smaller than her sister, even with the fuller curves that motherhood had given her, and this soft, silky robe tied loosely about her luscious body was out of an entirely different wardrobe.

'In the wash.'

Guilt welled up in Grace. If she'd been more careful….

'You did warn me,' she said, pulling free of the comfort of his arm. Comfort she didn't deserve. Then, palming away tears that were clinging to her lashes, 'I'm sorry. I'm trying so hard to hold it together, but I hadn't realised what it was like. Being a mother, totally responsible for a precious life, has nothing to do with whose egg made the baby, or even giving birth. This is what's real….'

'I know, Grace. I'm here.'

'You're here now,' she said. 'But what about next month? Next year…?'

It wasn't fair, she knew that, but she'd been struggling to settle Posie for what seemed like forever and was at her wits' end.

'I used to lie awake upstairs, listening to Posie cry in the night, and I actually envied my sister,' she confessed. 'I wanted to be the one to go to Posie, pick her up, comfort her.'

'That's perfectly natural, Grace.'

'No. You were right. I should have gone away.' She looked up at him. 'I saw the fear in Phoebe's eyes. Every time I picked her up. That's why I did everything I could to get the paperwork through so quickly.' She sighed. 'Be careful what you wish for, Josh.'

'You did not wish for this.'

'No.' She hadn't wished for this. 'I had no idea how alone new parents must feel. How frightened. She's so little, Josh. So vulnerable…'

'Hush…' For a moment she wasn't sure whether he was talking to the baby or to her. 'Try to relax—'

'Relax!' She shook her head. The baby was picking up her tension, they both knew it. 'I'm sorry. Shouting at you won't help.'

'Maybe we all need a good shout,' he said. 'But not right at this moment.' He lifted the baby from his shoulder, held her for a moment, kissed her head, then laid her in the crook of his arm and, taking the feeder from her, offered it to Posie.

She turned her head away.

'She won't take this, Grace.' Then, 'Maybe you should try feeding her yourself.'

'No…' She swallowed. 'No, Josh, I couldn't.'

Even as she said it, Posie started to grizzle again and, without saying another word, Josh took her hand and led her from the nursery and into her own bedroom.

'She wouldn't…'

'Just try,' he said.

'For Posie?' If it was for Posie, she could do it.

'For Posie. And for you, Grace.'

He pulled at the knot tying her robe and the silk slithered from her shoulders, leaving her standing in a thin nightgown that clung to her breasts, her legs, and she felt naked, exposed, in a way she hadn't on the night they'd made love and she let slip a little cry. Anguish. Heartache. Longing…

'Will you trust me?' he asked.

She looked up at him. With his tousled hair, the dark stubble of his chin, he didn't look like any baby guru, but yes, she would trust him with her life. He had been—was still—her hero. Her white knight. And she sat on the edge of the bed, eased herself back against the pillows.

'Ready?'

As soon as he'd laid the baby in her arms she began to cry and Grace instantly tensed again.

'Forget Posie,' he said, sitting on the edge of the bed, turning to her. 'Just relax. Let your shoulders drop.'

But she was shaking. Afraid. 'What if I can't do it?'

'You can.' And he laid his warm hands on her shoulders and began to gently knead the tension from knotted muscles, soothing, relaxing her so that her breathing became easier and the shivering stopped.

'Trust me,' he said, briefly laying his hand against her cheek, before letting it slide down her neck, slip beneath the thin strap of her nightgown.

She tried to speak, to protest, but the only sound that emerged was a tiny squeak from the back of her throat. The truth was that she couldn't have done or said a word to stop him. Didn't want to stop him….

Josh held his breath, knowing that they were both on the precipice of something special. Keeping his eyes fixed firmly on her face. She was wearing something soft, silky with narrow straps and he slipped one over her shoulder, let his hand slide down over the full, soft mound of her breast where once her nipple had hardened eagerly for him, as if begging for his touch.

But this was not a girl's breast. Not the small, high breast that tormented his dreams. It was full, womanly, filled his hand as he lifted it, bent to kiss it.

'Please…'

'Anything,' he said, his eyes never leaving hers, 'you said you would do anything.' And, seized by some atavistic need to make his own mark, he touched his tongue to her nipple.

It leapt in response and, feeling like some great hunter bringing home food for his tribe, he offered it to his baby.

Grace gasped as Posie's eager mouth found her nipple, fastened on. Groaned as she began to suckle and Josh, not knowing whether it was pain or joy that sent the tears cascading down her cheeks, took her face between his hands, brushing them away with his thumbs.

'This is for Posie, Grace,' he said, kissing each of her cheeks, tasting the salt on his lips. 'For your baby. Our baby.' And he silently swore to cherish them both for the rest of his life.

Grace, feeling closer to being a mother than she had since the cord had been cut, looked down at her baby who, eyes closed in ecstasy, fed with serene contentment.

'Well?' Josh asked.

'Very well…' She palmed away the stupid tears and smiled. 'How did you know?'

'Just call me Mr Spock,' he said.

'I think you mean *Dr* Spock,' she said, catching her lower lip to stop herself from laughing. And then she knew he'd done it deliberately, just as he had when she was still a kid and he was halfway to being a man. He'd always known what to do. When her dog had died, it was Josh who'd dug a grave for him at the bottom of the garden. Who'd carved his name into a piece of wood and hammered it into the ground. 'Thank you, Josh. I don't know what I'd have done without you.'

He touched her cheek. 'You'd have figured it out.' Then, 'Can I go and make you something to drink? Something milky to help you sleep?'

'I'll be fine now. But you must be exhausted,' she said, shuffling up to make more room beside her. 'Put your feet up.'

'I don't need much sleep,' he said, but he settled down beside her. 'I got up for some air. I'm used to being outside.'

'In your penthouse? On top of a skyscraper?' she teased.

'It has a deck.'

'Oh.'

'And a pool.'

'For goldfish?'

'For swimming.'

'Ouch.'

'No. You're right. It's wasted on me. I'm never there,' he said. He was never anywhere….

Posie stopped suckling, looked sleepily up at her. 'Had enough, baby?' she asked.

Her mouth began to work and Grace turned her round, jumped as she latched on to her other breast.

'Does that hurt?'

Her laugh was slightly shaky. 'Not hurt, but it does take your breath away for a moment or two. She's very strong.'

'I'm sure your mother would have something to say on the subject of the life force.'

Grace smiled. 'My mother has a lot to say about almost everything.'

Whereas Josh…

'I suppose you let friends use it when you're not there. The pool?' she said.

He glanced at her. 'Why would you think that?'

'Isn't that what people do?'

'Not if they've got an atom of sense,' he assured her. 'Besides, most of my friends have pools of their own.'

'In that case, maybe you should do something about your security because someone was there when I tried to get you on the phone.'

He frowned.

'Anna Carling?' she prompted. 'Your personal assistant?'

'Anna? Oh, right.'

Wrong, wrong, wrong!

'She wasn't actually in my apartment. My number is diverted to hers when I'm away.' Then, looking at her, 'Has that been bothering you?'

'No,' she said, much too quickly.

'She's a married woman, Grace.'

'Really?' And since when did that make any difference…?

'Married, with three grown-up kids and at least two grandchildren.'

'She didn't sound that old.'

'Grace?' When she wouldn't look at him, he leaned forward. 'You didn't think…'

'Stop it.'

'Of course you did.'

He was grinning while she was blushing like a girl. It wasn't as if she had any right to feel jealous, but when had that ever stopped her? She might have pitied the girls who Josh had dated way back when, but that hadn't stopped her hating every minute of every night he had been out with each one of them.

'You've never talked much about your life in Australia, Josh. Where you live. Your friends. Only about your work.'

'It's been my all-consuming passion,' he said.

'You've really never found anyone?'

'I found a lot of someones. They all suffered from the same problem.' He leaned across and kissed the frown from her forehead. 'They weren't you,' he said, yawning, settling lower into the bed. He muttered something else, then turned towards her, so that the entire length of his body, relaxed and fluid, seemed to mould itself to hers. His face against her naked breast, Posie's toes against his chin.

'Josh?' She stared down at him. His eyes were closed, but he couldn't be asleep. Not just like that. 'What did you say?'

No response. Jet lag had finally caught up with him and it would be cruel to disturb him. Instead, she turned to Posie. Her little girl was asleep, too, and she eased herself from beside Josh, put her back in her cot. Stood over her for a while before going back to bed.

Josh was dreaming again. It was the same dream that had haunted him for years. Grace, sensuous, silky, fragrant and forever—tormentingly—out of reach.

He turned, trying to escape the image, but it only made things worse. The scent so familiar, but warmer, closer. And the silky body so real beneath his hand that he could feel the slow beat of her pulse.

He opened his eyes and discovered that dreams really did come true. He was lying beside his sleeping love, his arm draped over her waist, her lips temptingly within kissing distance.

He resisted that temptation, knowing that once he kissed her she'd wake up, and this was a moment he never wanted to end. Then Posie woke and Grace opened her eyes.

Grace woke to the sound of Posie shouting joyfully from the nursery to let her know that it was time to get up. She lay for a moment, relishing the pleasure of a warm bed, the fact that she'd slept soundly, that the only weight pinning her down was Josh's hand on her hip.

Josh's hand.

And then she remembered.

What Josh had done. How, last night, when she'd been in despair, Josh had been there. Had made her truly a mother….

Had fallen asleep beside her.

She opened her eyes to look at him, only to find that he was watching her. That he hadn't just fallen asleep, but that he had stayed with her.

'Thank you,' she said.

He didn't answer, just gave her the sweetest kiss. A close-your-eyes-and-feel-the-tingle-in-your-toes kind of kiss. A first-kiss kind of kiss that was making her body do giddy little loop-the-loops.

And she knew that was where they had gone wrong. They hadn't started at the beginning but had gone for no-holds-barred, straight-to-hell passion. From here to eternity in one night. No words, all action.

He eased away to look at her. 'This is nice. Maybe we can do it again very soon?'

Now. Her body was screaming now and he was close

enough for her to be aware that he was heading the same way. But she wasn't making the same mistake again and, lifting her hand to his lips, she said, 'We need to talk, Josh. I have a thousand things to tell you.'

Or maybe only one....

'Now?'

Posie was shouting for attention and then her mother called up the stairs to let Josh know that his driver had arrived to take him to London. Even so, she knew that if she'd said yes, now, he would have stayed right where he was. But then there would be no conversation.

'It will keep,' she said. And then she returned his kiss with a sweet, soft touch of her lips to his. A promise that she would be waiting. Always.

CHAPTER ELEVEN

'YOU'RE getting married, Grace. I know you want a quiet, simple wedding and we all respect that, but you do have to have a new dress and the wedding is the day after tomorrow.'

'That's plenty of time to buy a dress.'

Grace saw her mother and Laura Kingsley exchange meaningful looks. Whoever would have thought those two would become bosom buddies? Arranging a wedding made strange bedfellows.

The thought made her smile.

'We had a look in that boutique in the craft centre the other day,' Laura said casually.

'The one next to the aromatherapy place. I needed some lavender oil,' her mother added, as if to establish the fact that they hadn't actually been *looking* for a dress.

'Yes?'

'Gorgeous clothes,' Laura said. 'I fell in love with a jacket. I think I might go back and get it today.' Then, 'They had a beautiful dress in your size.'

'Really? I didn't know they did large sizes…'

'Layers of different fabrics cut asymmetrically,' her mother continued, ignoring her attempt to distract them, force them into reassuring her that she wasn't fat.

'Simple but very stylish,' Laura added.

They made a great double act.

'Stylish sounds good,' she said, playing along. 'What colour?'

'It was cream.'

'Cream? Outsize and frumpy, then.'

'Did you have any particular colour in mind?' Laura asked, and she just knew that the pair of them had been through every shop in Maybridge and, whatever she said, they'd have an answer.

'I always thought that if I ever got married, I'd wear one of Geena Wagner's designs,' she said absently. 'She has a small showroom in a department store in Melchester, but her workroom is in the craft centre. She commissions me to make the tiaras to match her gowns. Have you seen her work, Laura?' Josh's mother was a fashion plate and probably knew every hot designer who could stitch a seam. 'She uses appliqué, embroidery and beading to stunning effect. One of her dresses was featured in a spread in *Celebrity* last year,' she added. 'With one of my tiaras.'

'Yes…' Laura cleared her throat. 'I believe I saw it. Quite lovely. But I think you've left it a little late to go for a hand-made designer dress.'

'She's a friend. And I wasn't thinking of anything elaborate. A simple ankle-length column dress with one of those little jackets that just covers the shoulders and arms?'

'Even so. These things take months…' Then, 'If you don't like cream—and I admit it can be very draining—what about peach? We did see something in peach, didn't we, Dawn?'

'Not white, you think?' Grace interjected, all innocence.

'Grace…' Her mother's eyes narrowed as she belatedly twigged to the fact that they were being teased.

'Sorry. I couldn't resist.'

Laura was looking from one to the other. 'Am I missing something?'

'I called Geena last week, Laura. When I went to check that Abby was still managing without me.' Which she was. Brilliantly.

It was the day she'd woken in Josh's arms and she'd known that they weren't just going to have a wedding, but a marriage.

They still had to talk, but she'd known, deep in her heart, that after that night, after what he'd done for her, it would never be just a marriage on paper. And she wanted, when she stood beside him and said the words that would make them man and wife, to show him that it really meant something to her. Wanted it to be a day that neither of them would ever forget.

'I'm going for a fitting today. In fact,' she said, making a point of looking at her watch, 'if you can be ready in twenty minutes, you can come with me.'

There was a moment of stunned silence and then a frantic scramble as the pair of them rushed to change. Well, Laura rushed. Her mother was slower, but just as determined.

She was still grinning to herself when the phone rang and she picked it up, knowing it would be Josh. He'd phoned her morning, noon and night while he'd been in London. He was later today.

'You're late this morning. Did you oversleep?' she asked, without preamble.

'I had an early meeting and didn't want to call you before six.'

'Good decision. How are you?'

'Busy. Lonely without my little girl. How is she?'

'Thriving. Sleeping through without any problems now.'

'Good. And the grannies?'

'I'm not asking and they're not telling, but your credit card—or maybe it's Laura—appears to have totally corrupted my mother.'

'I'm delighted to hear it. Sufficiently to give up her principles about jumping the queue and allowing me to pay for her hip replacement, do you think?'

'Oh, Josh…'

'I have to go, Grace. I'll call you later.'

'Later,' she repeated, but was talking to the dialling tone.

Josh smiled as he shut off his cellphone, pushing open the door to the kind of jewellery store that had been beyond his wildest dreams when he'd bought that first ring for Grace.

Something unusual, antique, he thought. Emeralds to match her eyes….

He'd just handed over his credit card when his phone rang.

Still haunted by the thought that he might have missed a call from Michael, missing Grace's call, he moved away from the desk to check the caller.

It was his Chinese partner calling from Beijing. He let the call go to voicemail while he punched in his pin code. He wasn't due back in Maybridge until tomorrow, but he planned to surprise Grace, take her out, ask her to marry him. Be his wife.

'Congratulations, sir. I hope you'll be very happy,' the jeweller said as he handed him the ring.

His smile lasted until he was in the back of his limousine, when he listened to the frantic voicemail, the you-have-to-be-here-tomorrow bureaucratic foul-up that he couldn't ignore. It was his responsibility and his alone. He'd signed a contract. There were billions of dollars, thousands of jobs at stake.

He could call Grace, explain, put off the wedding until he could get back. She'd understand. But what would it be next time? How long would it be before he could get back to see Posie again? Months. She'd have grown, changed, forgotten him. And that was how it would be through all the years. He wouldn't be a father, or a husband in anything but name. He'd be the stranger who turned up once in a blue moon, when it fitted in with his plans.

And he thought about what Dawn had told him to ask himself. Who gained, who would be hurt by the choices he made? But it was the latter that was important. Whose happiness you truly cared about.

He didn't, he discovered, have to agonise over that one. He knew.

It was late, long after Josh would normally have phoned, when a courier arrived with a package addressed to Grace and she knew—just knew—that whatever it contained she didn't want to know.

She shut herself in the study and opened the envelope. The letter inside was handwritten, brief and to the point:

Grace,

By the time you receive this I will be on my way to Beijing. It seems that you were right all along. I was fitting in our wedding, not because I was making time for it, but because it fitted in with my own schedule, just as I would fit Posie into my life.

I asked your mother how you knew what was the right to decision to make. She told me that if I was honest with myself it would be clear. It's time to be honest and admit that my life is not one that lends itself to either marriage or fatherhood. Posie is your child in every conceivable way and it is right and proper that you should have full care of her.

Enclosed with this letter you will find a copy of my instructions to Michael's lawyer that he should apply to the courts for a Parental Responsibility Order on your behalf. If you wish, later, to formally adopt Posie, I will make no objection.

I will, of course, stand by my agreement to buy the house once Probate is granted. Arrangements have also been made for the estate to pay a maintenance allowance for Posie and you as her carer, as well as any other necessary expenses.

I have no idea when I will return to Sydney, but if you need any further help in the future please contact Anna Carling. She has been instructed to treat any request from you as if it were my own.

Yours, Josh

'Why?' She waved the letter at her mother. 'Why is he doing this? What did you say to him?'

Her mother said nothing.

Laura looked as if she might say something but, when Grace turned on her, she shook her head. Then, 'He was marrying you to keep Posie? Why would he do that?'

'Because she is his daughter, Laura. Our daughter. My egg, his sperm…'

'Oh.' Then, 'But…' She shook her head. 'I don't understand any of it.'

'I think I do,' her mother said. 'It's a sacrifice move.'

'Sacrifice?'

'He's giving her up, surrendering her to you.'

'What?'

'We talked about it. About love. The choices you make. Holding on. Letting go. Whether you loved enough to let go even when it felt like tearing your heart out of your body.' Then, 'I think he just did that, Grace. Tore out his heart and gave it to you.'

Grace said something completely out of character. 'He's giving up his daughter just because he had to fly off to Beijing and sort out some emergency and miss a ten minute ceremony in a *folly*? What kind of idiot is he?'

'I'm sorry. It never occurred to me… I thought…'

She shook her head. 'No, Mum, this isn't your fault. It's mine. I kept telling him he wasn't committed, that he'd never be here for Posie, when I should have been telling him that I love him.' She got up, walked to the phone. Picked it up. 'Clinging to my safe little nest instead of telling him that wherever he was I wanted to be, too.'

'Who are you calling?'

She stared at the phone. 'Good point. Who do you call when you want to book an airline ticket?'

'The Internet?'

'Right.'

'Where are you going?' Laura asked.

'Where do you think? Bei-flipping-jing.'

'Why don't you let me do that?' her mother said, taking the phone from her and replacing it. 'While you go and pack.'

'Two seats,' she said, backing out of the room. 'Or whatever they have for babies. On the first available flight.'

Her mother, flipping through the telephone directory, stopped. 'You can't take Posie.'

'I have to. I'm breastfeeding…'

'But you haven't got a passport for her.'

For a moment the world seemed to stand still. Then she said, 'Phoebe had. They were going to France this summer…'

Josh swiped the key to his suite and walked in, desperate for a shower, a drink, sleep.

It was finally sorted. Something or nothing that would have been fixed in ten minutes in Australia had required delicate diplomacy, tact, face-saving manoeuvres, when one phrase in a contract had been incorrectly translated.

He opened the mini-bar, took out a Scotch, put it back and took out a bottle of water instead.

His body was in enough trouble without adding alcohol to the mix.

He tossed his jacket on the sofa, loosened his tie, opened the bedroom door and stopped. When he'd left it, this room had contained nothing except the carry-on grip he used when travelling.

Now there was a bright pink holdall, a box of disposable nappies, a very familiar buggy and a cot had been set up at the foot of the bed. The cot contained a sleeping Posie and in the bed Grace lay, fully dressed, flat on her back with her arms thrown out.

Grace?

It couldn't be. The longing, the need, the unbelievable loneliness were inducing hallucinations.

He closed his eyes. Opened them again. She was still there but, needing to convince himself that she was real, he put out a hand and very gently, so as not to wake her, touched her cheek. Then kissed her just as gently.

No illusion, but warm, real flesh.

Grace, who never went anywhere, who had made herself sick rather than go on a school trip to France, had flown half-way round the world to… What? He'd given her everything she wanted.

He turned to Posie. She was lying exactly like her mother. Flat on her back, arms flung wide.

He didn't think he could bear it.

He wanted to hold them both, tell them how much he'd missed them, how much he loved them. But he'd made his decision and, leaving them to sleep, he shut himself in the bathroom, showered as quietly as he could, half expecting that when he opened the door, they would have disappeared.

He was half right. Posie was still asleep, but the bed was empty and he walked through to the living room where Grace was signing the bill for room service.

'I tried not to wake you,' he said.

'Kissing a girl when you've got a beard is not something

you can do without repercussions, Josh,' she said, as she poured two cups of tea. Helped herself to a sandwich.

'You're not giving me much of an incentive to shave it off, Grace. I thought you'd be asleep for hours. Why are you here?'

'You have to ask? You bailed out on our talk, Josh. The one we were going to have about the future, about us. And you bailed out on our wedding, too. Okay. It happens. You walked out on me after the most incredible, most perfect night of my life and I should have been ready for you to cut and run again.'

Perfect?

'If it had just been me,' Grace went on, 'I could have lived with it. I've lived without the man I love for ten years so the rest of my life would be a breeze. But I'm here to tell you that I don't believe you'd run out on your daughter, Joshua Kingsley.'

'Ten years?' He shook his head. That didn't make sense. The fact that she was here didn't make sense. 'I did what I thought was for the best, Grace,' he said.

'I'm here to tell you that you're wrong. And that I'm really tired of you leaving before the credits have rolled. Before I can tell you that I love you. That I've always loved you. You're an impossible act to follow, Josh Kingsley.'

There. She'd said it. It was over. And, right on cue, Posie woke up and began to chatter to herself.

'Your daughter is awake, Josh,' she said, getting up and walking back into the bedroom. 'I've left a couple of feeders of breast milk in the fridge to keep you going until you can buy some formula and there are enough nappies to keep you going for a day or two. Anna is interviewing nannies.' She picked up the pink holdall and began to walk to the door.

'Grace?'

She didn't stop. Didn't turn round.

'Where are you going?'

'Home,' she said, not missing a stride. 'I've done what I came for. I've brought you your daughter.'

'No!'

She reached the door.

'Please, Grace.'

Opened it.

'I love you.'

She let out the breath she'd been holding but still didn't turn round.

'I've always loved you. I came back that first year with a ring in my pocket.'

'No…' That couldn't be true. He'd scarcely looked at her. 'No,' she said, turning to face him. 'You never called. Never wrote. Not even a postcard.'

'I meant to, but I didn't know what to say. Sorry? Thank you? There was only one thing you'd want to hear and I couldn't write it.'

Plain and honest… She was certainly getting what she'd asked for.

'So why the ring?'

'I couldn't face you without it and then, having screwed myself to the sticking point, admitted that I wanted you, I discovered that you'd found someone else.'

'And you just accepted that? Didn't bother to put up a fight? Josh Kingsley, who always got what he went after?'

'I was…relieved.'

'Off the hook, you mean. That wasn't love, Josh. That was guilt. And you were married to Jessie within a year. Still, when you've got a ring…'

'I didn't give Jessie your ring. I threw it in the bin, then I realised that Phoebe would find it, so I took it out again. I still have it.'

She shook her head, not wanting to believe it.

'It's in my apartment in Sydney. At the back of my sock drawer.'

'No…'

It was a cry from the heart for everything she'd lost and in a second he was there beside her, his arms around her, but she had to tell him. Now. This minute, before her heart shattered.

'There was never anyone else, Josh. There has never been anyone else. They were all just camouflage. You'd left me and I didn't want you to know how much that had hurt me. One word. If you'd just said one word…'

'I was afraid. I thought you'd slow me down.'

She looked up at him. 'You were right.'

'Was I? Truly? If I'd had an ounce of your strength, purpose, if I'd had the courage to tell you that I loved you, you would have braved anything to come with me.'

She shook her head, but he caught her chin, forced her to look at him.

'It's true. How did you do it now, Grace? Where did you find the strength to fly into the unknown?'

'Love,' she said. 'Your love, your sacrifice gave me wings.'

'And now you're prepared to do the same?'

'Actually, Josh, I was banking on the fact that having done it yourself, you'd finally get the message.'

'Tell me anyway.'

'"…whither thou goest, I will go; and where thou lodgest, I will lodge…" We're a family, Josh. It doesn't matter where we are, so long as we're together.'

Josh felt as if his heart were bursting. He'd given everything and in return he'd gained the world.

'There's just one more question,' he said. 'Will you marry me? Not a paper marriage, but a making babies, till-death-us-do part, forever and a day marriage. In a wedding with flowers and bridesmaids and doves and string quartets. I'll even shave off the beard.'

'No,' she said. Then, while his heart was still recovering from the shock, 'No doves, no string quartets and I'll take a rain check on the beard until I've road-tested it.' Then, when he just grinned, 'That's a hint, Josh. We've got ten years to catch up on.'

From the Maybridge Gazette:

DUCKS ADD DELIGHT
AND DRAMA TO WEDDING

Local businesswoman Grace McAllister and Maybridge-born tycoon Joshua Kingsley were married today in a charmingly simple ceremony in the folly at Melchester Castle.

The bride wore a Geena Wagner gown in ivory silk with a matching high-collared bolero that had been appliquéd and embroidered in shades of green and turquoise. Her matching tiara was designed and made by the bride's business partner, Abby Green.

The couple's niece, Posie Kingsley, and the groom's half-sisters, Lucy, Alice and Maude Kingsley were bridesmaids.

The ceremony was followed by a country picnic for family and friends beside the lake where the guests were entertained by a traditional fiddler, folk singers and morris dancing. A dozen white ducks, decked out in emerald bows, added rural charm to the scene, but during the afternoon they escaped their handler and made for the lake. So far all attempts to capture them have failed.

The couple, who have now left on an extended honeymoon that reportedly includes India, the United States and Japan, have homes in Maybridge and Sydney, Australia,

* * * * *

*Celebrate 60 years of pure reading pleasure with
Harlequin®!*

*Step back in time and enjoy a sneak preview of an exciting
anthology from Harlequin® Historical with*
THE DIAMONDS OF WELBOURNE MANOR

This compelling anthology features three stories about
the outrageous Fitzmanning sisters. Meet Annalise, who
is never at a loss for words… But that can change with
an unexpected encounter in the forest.

Available May 2009 from Harlequin® Historical.

"I'm the illegitimate daughter of notoriously scandalous parents, Mr. Milford. Candidates for my hand are unlikely to be lining up at the gates."

"Don't be so quick to discount your charms, my dear. Or the charm of your substantial dowry. Or even your brothers' influence. There are as many reasons to marry as there are marriages."

Annalise snorted. "Oh, yes. Perhaps I shall marry for dynastic reasons, or perhaps for property or influence. After all, a loveless, practical marriage worked out so well for my mother."

"Well, you've routed me on that one. I can think of no suitable rejoinder." Ned rose to his feet and extended his hand. "And since that is the case, let me be the first to wish you a long and happy spinsterhood."

Her mouth gaped open. And then she laughed.

And he froze.

This was the first time, Ned realized. The first time he'd seen her eyes light up and her mouth curl. The first time he'd witnessed her features melded together in glorious accord to produce exquisite beauty.

Unbelievable what a change came over her face. Unheard of what effect her throaty, rasping laughter had on his body. It pounded a beat upon his ear, quickly taken up by his pulse. It echoed through him, finally residing in his stirring nether regions.

So easily she did it, awakened these sensations within him—without any apparent effort at all. And she had called him potentially dangerous? Clearly the intelligent thing for him to do would be to steer clear, to leave her to the tender ministrations of Lord Peter Blackthorne.

"You were right." She smiled up at him as she took his hand and climbed to her feet. "I do feel better."

Ah, well. When had he ever chosen the intelligent path?

He did not relinquish her hand. He used it to pull her in, close enough that he could feel the warmth of her. "At the risk of repeating Lord Peter's mistake and anticipating too much—may I ask if you'll be my partner in battledore tomorrow?"

Her smiled dimmed. Her breath came a little faster. His own had gone shallow, as if he'd just run a race—and lost. He ran his gaze over the appealing lift of her brow and the curious angle of her chin. His index finger twitched.

"I should like that," she said.

His finger trembled again and he lifted it, traced the pink and tender shell of her ear, the unique sweep of her jaw. Her pulse leaped beneath her skin, triggering his own. Slowly he tilted her chin up, waiting for her to object, to step back, to slap his hand away.

She did none of those eminently sensible things. Which left him free to do the entirely impractical thing.

Baby soft, the skin of her lips. Her whole body trembled when he touched her there.

He leaned in. Her eyes closed, even as she stood straight against him, strung as tight as a bow. He pressed his mouth to hers. It was a soft kiss, sweet and chaste. And yet he was hot and hard and as ready as he'd ever been in his life.

She drew back a little. Sighed. Their breath mingled a moment before she slowly backed away.

"Oh," she breathed. Her dark eyes were full of wonder and

something that looked like fear. He took a step toward her, but she only shook her head. His outstretched hand fell to his side as she turned to disappear into the wood. This was the first time, Ned realized. The first time, since he'd come to the house party at Welbourne Manor, that he'd seen her eyes light up.

* * * * *

Follow Ned and Annalise's story in May 2009 in
THE DIAMONDS OF WELBOURNE MANOR
Available May 2009 from Harlequin® Historical

Available in the series romance section,
or in the historical romance section,
wherever books are sold.

We'll be spotlighting a different series
every month throughout 2009
to celebrate our 60th anniversary.

Look for Harlequin® Historical in May!

Celebrations begin with
a sumptuous Regency house party!

Join three scandalous sisters in

**THE DIAMONDS OF
WELBOURNE MANOR**

Glittering, scintillating, sensual fun
by Diane Gaston, Deb Marlowe
and Amanda McCabe.

**60 years of Harlequin,
600 years of romance
in Harlequin Historical!**

Return to Virgin River with a breathtaking
new trilogy from award-winning author

ROBYN CARR

| February 2009 | March 2009 | April 2009 |

"The Virgin River books are so compelling—
I connected instantly with the characters
and just wanted more and more and more."
—#1 *New York Times* bestselling author
Debbie Macomber

MIRA®

HARLEQUIN® *Romance*®

Our

ON BOARD

miniseries has grown!

Now you can share in even more
tears and triumphs as
Harlequin Romance® brings you
a month full of

**Pregnancy and Proposals,
Miracles and Marriage!**

*Available in May
wherever books are sold.*

The Inside Romance newsletter has a NEW look for the new year!

Same great content, brand-new look!

The Inside Romance newsletter is a FREE quarterly newsletter highlighting our upcoming series releases and promotions!

Click on the Inside Romance link on the front page of **www.eHarlequin.com** or e-mail us at insideromance@harlequin.ca to sign up to receive your FREE newsletter today!

You can also subscribe by writing to us at: HARLEQUIN BOOKS Attention: Customer Service Department P.O. Box 9057, Buffalo, NY 14269-9057

Please allow 4-6 weeks for delivery of the first issue by mail.

IRNNEW09

REQUEST YOUR FREE BOOKS!
2 FREE NOVELS PLUS 2
FREE GIFTS!

HARLEQUIN ROMANCE®

From the Heart, For the Heart

YES! Please send me 2 FREE Harlequin Romance® novels and my 2 FREE gifts (gifts are worth about $10). After receiving them, if I don't wish to receive any more books, I can return the shipping statement marked "cancel". If I don't cancel, I will receive 4 brand-new novels every month and be billed just $3.32 per book in the U.S. or $3.80 per book in Canada, plus 25¢ shipping and handling per book and applicable taxes, if any*. That's a savings of over 15% off the cover price! I understand that accepting the 2 free books and gifts places me under no obligation to buy anything. I can always return a shipment and cancel at any time. Even if I never buy another book, the two free books and gifts are mine to keep forever.

114 HDN ERQW 314 HDN ERQ9

Name _____ (PLEASE PRINT) _____

Address _____ Apt. # _____

City _____ State/Prov. _____ Zip/Postal Code _____

Signature (if under 18, a parent or guardian must sign)

Mail to the **Harlequin Reader Service:**
IN U.S.A.: P.O. Box 1867, Buffalo, NY 14240-1867
IN CANADA: P.O. Box 609, Fort Erie, Ontario L2A 5X3

Not valid to current subscribers of Harlequin Romance books.

Want to try two free books from another line?
Call 1-800-873-8635 or visit www.morefreebooks.com.

* Terms and prices subject to change without notice. N.Y. residents add applicable sales tax. Canadian residents will be charged applicable provincial taxes and GST. Offer not valid in Quebec. This offer is limited to one order per household. All orders subject to approval. Credit or debit balances in a customer's account(s) may be offset by any other outstanding balance owed by or to the customer. Please allow 4 to 6 weeks for delivery. Offer available while quantities last.

Your Privacy: Harlequin Books is committed to protecting your privacy. Our Privacy Policy is available online at www.eHarlequin.com or upon request from the Reader Service. From time to time we make our lists of customers available to reputable third parties who may have a product or service of interest to you. If you would prefer we not share your name and address, please check here. ☐

HR08R

You're invited to join our Tell Harlequin Reader Panel!

By joining our new reader panel you will:

- Receive Harlequin® books—they are FREE and yours to keep with no obligation to purchase anything!
- Participate in fun online surveys
- Exchange opinions and ideas with women just like you
- Have a say in our new book ideas and help us publish the best in women's fiction

In addition, you will have a chance to win great prizes and receive special gifts! See Web site for details. Some conditions apply. Space is limited.

To join, visit us at
www.TellHarlequin.com.

Coming Next Month

Available May 12, 2009

Next month, Harlequin Romance® brings you
pregnancy and proposals, motherhood and marriage!
And don't forget to make a date with the second book
in our brand-new trilogy, *www.blinddatebrides.com!*

#4093 ADOPTED: FAMILY IN A MILLION Barbara McMahon
Baby on Board
Searching for his adopted son, Zack discovers sexy single mom Susan.
But she has no idea how inextricably their paths are linked....

#4094 HIRED: NANNY BRIDE Cara Colter
Baby on Board
On meeting playboy tycoon Joshua, nanny Dannie begins to see that
there is more to the man than designer suits. She wishes he could see
the real her, too.

#4095 ITALIAN TYCOON, SECRET SON Lucy Gordon
Baby on Board
Disaster brought Mandy love when she was stranded in an avalanche
with gorgeous Italian Renzo. But a year later, will he still want to claim
her—and their son?

#4096 BLIND-DATE BABY Fiona Harper
www.blinddatebrides.com
After finding love with handsome stranger Noah when her daughter
signs her up for an Internet-dating site, it's time for flirty forty-year-old
Grace to embrace motherhood once again!

#4097 THE BILLIONAIRE'S BABY Nicola Marsh
Baby on Board
Billionaire Blane wants the only thing money can't buy—to win back his
wife, Cam. As he romances her under the sizzling Australian sun, will
their spark reignite?

#4098 DOORSTEP DADDY Shirley Jump
Baby on Board
Writer Dalton demands solitude, not a baby on his doorstep! But when
single mom Ellie and her baby come into his life, it's time for Dalton to
start a whole new chapter....